Dedalus European Classics
General Editor: Timothy Lane

As Trains Pass By

(Katinka)

Herman Bang

AS
TRAINS PASS BY
(KATINKA)

Translated by W. Glyn Jones

Dedalus

Dedalus would like to thank The Danish Arts Council's Committee for Literature and Arts Council England, London for their assistance in publishing this book.

Published in the UK by Dedalus Limited,
24-26, St Judith's Lane, Sawtry, Cambs, PE28 5XE
email: info@dedalusbooks.com
www.dedalusbooks.com

ISBN printed book 978 1 909232 92 1
ISBN ebook 978 1 910213 09 4

Dedalus is distributed in the USA & Canada by SCB Distributors,
15608 South New Century Drive, Gardena, CA 90248
email: info@scbdistributors.com   web: www.scbdistributors.com

Dedalus is distributed in Australia by Peribo Pty Ltd.
58, Beaumont Road, Mount Kuring-gai, N.S.W. 2080
email: info@peribo.com.au

Publishing History
First published in Denmark in 1886
First Dedalus edition in 2015
First ebook edition in 2015

As Trains Pass By (Katinka) translation copyright © W. Glyn Jones 2014

The right of W. Glyn Jones to be identified as the translator of this work has been asserted by him in accordance with the Copyright, Designs and Patents Act, 1988.

Printed in Finland by Bookwell
Typeset by Marie Lane

A C.I.P. listing for this book is available on request.

This book is dedicated to the memory of W. Glyn Jones who died shortly after completing this translation.

He was a fine translator and a passionate advocate for Danish Literature.

The Author

Herman Bang (1857–1912) was from an aristocratic Danish family. His homosexuality led to a smear campaign against him and his exclusion from Danish literary circles. He worked as a theatre producer and as a journalist, having first tried unsuccessfully to be an actor.

His first novel *Families Without Hope* was banned for obscenity. He specialised in novels about isolated female characters, including *Ida Brandt* and *As Trains Pass By (Katinka)*.

The Translator

W. Glyn Jones (1928–2014) had a distinguished career as an academic, a writer and a translator.

He taught at various universities in England and Scandinavia before becoming Professor of Scandinavian Studies at Newcastle and then at the University of East Anglia. He also spent two years as Professor of Scandinavian Literature in the Faeroese Academy. On his retirement from teaching he was created a Knight of the Royal Danish Order of the Dannebrog.

He has written widely on Danish, Faeroese and Finland-Swedish literature. He is the the author of *Denmark: A Modern History* and co-author with his wife, Kirsten Gade, of *Colloquial Danish* and the *Blue Guide to Denmark*.

W. Glyn Jones' many translations from Danish include *Seneca* by Villy Sorensen and for Dedalus *The Black Cauldron*, *The Lost Musicians*, *Windswept Dawn*, *The Good Hope* and *Mother Pleiades* by William Heinesen, *Ida Brandt* and *As Trains Pass By (Katinka)* by Herman Bang and *My Fairy-Tale Life* by Hans Christian Andersen.

From Herman Bang's own introduction:

It was a couple of years ago in the north of Jutland. I had been giving a reading the previous evening in a town up there and this evening I was to give one in another town. I was tired; the train was moving slowly, as our expresses do, and there was no end to the journey.

Now we had stopped again. We came to a halt every five minutes.

I rose in my seat to see how many miles we still had to go, when my eye wandered from the sign beneath the station roof and fell on one of the green-framed windows.

This window was crammed with an abundance of rare flowers: palms and flowering cacti. And from among these flowers – its chin resting on two slender, white hands – a pale face was staring out at the train with the large, shiny eyes of a sick person. This young woman made no move. Quietly, with her head resting on her hands, she simply stared out at the line as long as I could see her.

Throughout my journey after that I saw this woman's face in the midst of her flowers. Her gaze scarcely suggested longing – *longing* had perhaps fluttered its wings until it died by beating them against those constricting walls – but merely quiet resignation, silent sorrow.

And when the train had glided past, she would once more stare out in the same position and with the same look, across the heather-covered landscape, out across the wide and monotonous countryside.

I

The stationmaster put on his uniform coat to be ready for the train.

"There's no damn time for anything," he said, stretching his arms. He had been dozing over the accounts.

He lit a cigar stub and went out onto the platform. Now, as he walked up and down, erect in his uniform and with his hands in both his jacket pockets, there was still something of the lieutenant about him. And it could be seen in his legs, too, which were still bent in the way they had been in the cavalry.

Five or six farm lads had arrived and were standing (legs akimbo) in a group opposite the station building; the station porter dragged the freight out, a single green-painted chest that looked as though it had been dropped by the side of the road.

The parson's daughter, tall as an officer in the guards, flung the platform gate open and entered.

The stationmaster clicked his heels and saluted.

"And what does madam intend to do today?" he said. When he was "on the platform", the stationmaster conversed in the tone he used to employ in the club balls at Næstved in his old cavalry days.

"Walk," said the parson's daughter. She made some curious flapping gestures as she spoke, as though she intended to hit whoever she was addressing.

"By the way, Miss Abel is coming home."

"Already – from town?"

"Ye-es."

"Nothing in the offing yet?" The stationmaster extended the fingers on his right hand in the air, and the parson's daughter laughed.

"Here come the family," she said. "I made my excuses and ran away from them…"

The stationmaster paid his respects to the Abel family, the widowed Mrs Abel and her elder daughter Louise. They were accompanied by Miss Jensen. Mrs Abel looked resigned.

"Yes," she said, "I have come to meet my younger daughter Ida."

Mrs Abel took it in turns to fetch her Louise and her younger daughter Ida. Louise in the spring and her younger daughter Ida in the autumn.

They each spent six weeks with an aunt in Copenhagen. "My sister, the one who was married to a State Councillor," said Mrs Abel. The State Councillor's widow resided in a fourth floor apartment and made a living by decorating terracotta ornaments with paintings of storks standing on one leg. Mrs Abel always dispatched her daughters with many good wishes.

She had now been dispatching them for ten years.

"And such letters we have received from my younger daughter this time."

"Aye, those letters," said Miss Jensen.

"But it is better to have your chicks at home," said Mrs Abel, looking tenderly at Louise. Mrs Abel had to dry her eyes at the thought.

The six months they were at home, Mrs Abel's chicks spent quarrelling and sewing fresh trimmings on old dresses. They never spoke to their mother.

"How could one possibly live in an out-of-the-way place

like this if one did not have a family life?" said the widow.

Miss Jensen nodded.

There came the sound of barking from the corner over by the inn, and a coach appeared.

"That's the Kiærs," said the parson's daughter. "What can they want?"

She went across the platform to the gate.

"Aye," Kiær, the gentleman farmer, got out of his carriage. "You might well ask. Now Madsen's gone and caught typhoid just at the worst possible time, so I've had to wire for a replacement and God knows what kind of rubbish I'm going to get. He's due here now."

Mr Kiær came onto the platform.

"He's been to the Royal College of Agriculture, if that means anything, and he got top marks there as well. Oh, good morning, Bai." The station master was allowed to shake hands. "You look a bit bleary-eyed. How's the wife?"

"Fine, thank you. So you're here to fetch a new bailiff."

"Aye, dreadful story, and just at the worst possible time."

"Oh a new man in the district," says the parson's daughter waving her arms about as though she was already giving him a box on the ears. "With Wee Bentzen the porter that means six and a half."

The widow was suddenly all of a flutter. She had said it at home: her elder daughter Louise was not to go out wearing those prunella boots.

Her feet were the source of her elder daughter Louise's beauty: slender, aristocratic feet.

And she had told her.

Miss Louise was in the waiting room adjusting her veil. The young Abels went in for low-cut dresses with ruffs, jet beads and veils.

Bai went indoors to the kitchen to tell his wife about the bailiff. The parson's daughter sat swinging her legs on the green-painted chest. She took out her watch and checked the time. "Good heavens, that man's certainly making us wait," she said.

Miss Jensen said, "Yes, the train seems to be an appreciable number of minutes late." Miss Jensen spoke indescribably correctly, especially when talking to the parson's daughter.

She did not approve of the parson's daughter.

"That is not the tone to be used by my pupils," she said to the widow. Miss Jensen was not entirely sure in her use of foreign words.

"But there we have our lovely lady." The parson's daughter bounced up from the chest and rushed across the platform towards Mrs Bai, who had appeared on the stone steps. When the parson's daughter gave someone a hearty greeting, it looked as though she was about to commit a violent assault.

Mrs Bai smiled quietly and allowed herself to be kissed.

"Heaven help us," said the parson's daughter, "we're unexpectedly going to have a new cock on the midden. Here he comes!"

They heard the sound of the train in the distance and the loud clattering as it crossed the bridge over the river. Swaying and puffing, it made its slow approach across the meadow.

The parson's daughter remained on the steps, holding Mrs Bai around the waist.

"That's Ida Abel," said the parson's daughter. "I know her by her veil." A Bordeaux-coloured veil emerged from a window.

The train stopped, and doors were opened and closed. Mrs Abel shouted her "Hello" in such a loud voice that the occupants of all the nearby compartments came to the windows.

The younger daughter Ida squeezed her mother's arm angrily; she was still standing on the step:

"There's a gentleman on the train – coming here."

"Who is he?" Everything was going nineteen to the dozen.

Ida was down on the platform. There was the gentleman, a very staid-looking, fair-haired gentleman with a beard who was taking a hat box and cases out of a smoking compartment.

"And Auntie, Auntie Mi," shouted the widow.

"Shush," said her younger daughter Ida in a quiet but irate voice. "Where's Louise?"

Louise turned and sprang like a child up the stone steps in front of Mrs Bai and the parson's daughter, as though her "beauty" resided in her button boots.

At the bottom of the steps, the bailiff made himself known to Mr Kiær.

"Aye, the devil of a story. There's Madsen in bed, at the very worst time. Ah well, we'll hope for the best." Mr Kiær slapped the new bailiff on the shoulder.

"Heaven preserve us," said the parson's daughter. "A very ordinary domestic animal."

The green-painted box was in the train and the cans for the cooperative dairy had been hoisted onto the goods wagon. The train was just starting to move when a farmer shouted out of a window: he had no ticket.

The guard, a smart young man as straight as a hussar briefly touched hands with Bai and jumped up onto the running board.

The farmer continued to shout and argue with the guard, who was still hanging on to the running board.

And for a moment all faces on the platform turned towards the train as it rumbled away.

"Hmm, and that was that," said the parson's daughter. She went into the entrance hall with Mrs Bai.

"My bailiff, Mr. Huus," said Mr Kiær in the direction of Bai as he was about to walk past. The three stood there for a moment.

Louise and young Ida finally found each other and started kissing madly in the doorway.

"Oh, good heavens," said the widow, "they haven't seen each other for six weeks."

"You are fortunate, Mr Huus," said Bai in his club-ball voice. "You can make the acquaintance of the ladies of this place without further ado. Ladies, may I introduce you?"

The Misses Abel interrupted their kissing as though on command.

"The Misses Abel," said Mr Bai. "Mr Huus."

"Yes, I have just come to meet my younger daughter – from Copenhagen," said the widow out of the blue.

"Mrs Abel," said Mr Bai.

Mr Huus bowed.

"Miss Linde" (This was the parson's daughter.) "Mr Huus."

The parson's daughter inclined her head.

"And my wife," said Bai.

Mr Huus said a few words, and then they all went in to fetch their luggage.

Farmer Kiær drove off with the bailiff. The others walked. When they reached the road, they discovered they had forgotten Miss Jensen.

She still stood on the platform, dreaming away, leaning against a signal post.

"Miss Jensen," the parson's daughter yelled from the road.

Miss Jensen started. Miss Jensen always came over melancholy when she saw a railway. She could not abide to see "anything leaving".

"Seems to be a really nice person," said Mrs Abel as they

walked along the road.

"Very ordinary bailiff," said the parson's daughter; she was walking arm in arm with Mrs Bai. "He had nice hands."

The two chicks tailed along at the end of the group, bickering.

"I must say, Miss Jensen, you are in a hurry," said the parson's daughter. Miss Jensen was far ahead of them, jumping the puddles like a goat. She was making a considerable show of her maidenly legs on account of the autumnal humidity.

They walked by the tiny woodland. At the turn of the road, Mrs Bai said goodbye.

"Oh, you look so tiny and natty in that big shawl. What a lovely lady!" said the parson's daughter, reaching out as though to embrace her.

"Goodbye."

"Goo-oo-d bye"

"She'll never be out of breath with the amount she says," said young Ida.

The parson's daughter whistled.

"Oh, there's the curate," said Mrs Abel. "Good evening, curate. Good evening."

The curate raised his hat. "I had to say good evening to Ida as she returned home," he said.

"Well, Miss Abel. Are you in good health?"

"Yes, thank you," said Miss Abel.

"And you have received a competitor, curate," said Mrs Abel.

"Oh? Where?"

"Kiær was fetching his new bailiff. A very attractive person. Wasn't he, Miss Linde?"

"Oh yes."

"First rate, Miss Linde?"

"Top hole," said the parson's daughter.

The parson's daughter and the curate always spoke in a kind of jargon when they were together with others, and they never uttered a word of sense. They laughed at their own foolishness until they were almost fit to burst.

The parson's daughter no longer went to church when the curate was preaching since one Sunday when she had almost made him laugh as he was standing in the pulpit reciting the Lord's Prayer.

"Miss Jensen rushed off as though she had rockets in a certain part of her anatomy," said the curate.

Miss Jensen was still ahead of them.

"Oh, Andersen," Miss Linde laughed heartily, "now you sound like Holberg."

They reached the parsonage, which was the first house in the village, and the parson's daughter and the curate took leave of the others at the garden gate.

"Goodbye, Miss Jensen," shouted Miss Linde down the road. Miss Jensen answered her with a squeak.

"What was he like?" said the curate when in the garden. His tone was quite different now.

"Oh, good heavens," said Miss Linde, "a very ordinary farmer."

Silently, they walked side by side down through the garden.

"Hmm," said Miss Ida. The Abel family caught up with Miss Jensen, who was standing waiting for them on some dry ground, "I am sure he had come to say good morning to me."

They walked on a little. Then Miss Jensen said:

"There are so many different kinds of people."

"Yes," said Mrs Abel.

"I am not happy when I am together with that family," said Miss Jensen. "I prefer to avoid them."

Miss Jensen had "avoided them" for a week since the vicar had said all those things.

"Mrs Abel," said Miss Jensen, "who pays any heed to an unmarried lady? I said so to the vicar: 'Vicar,' I said, 'you are interested in the Free School, so parents send their children to the Free School.' And what was his answer to me, Mrs Abel? 'I will not discuss the question of scholarships with Mr Linde any more. The parish council has removed half the scholarship money from my institute (Miss Jensen put the stress on the final syllable), but I will continue to do my duty even if they take the other half as well. I will not discuss the scholarship question with Mr Linde any further.' "

The three ladies turned into the little road leading up to the "hall", an old building with two wings.

Mrs Abel lived in the wing on the right, and Miss Jensen's institute was in that on the left.

"How nice to have them both with me again," said the widow. They took leave of each other in the courtyard.

"Ugh," said young Ida once they were inside the door, "you two looked such a mess at the station, I was ashamed of you."

"I wonder how you expect me to look," said Louise as she took off her veil before the looking glass, "when you have all the clothes."

The widow put on some slippers. The soles of her boots were worn out.

Miss Jensen finally extracted the key from her pocket and let herself in. In the sitting room, the pug gave a couple of irritated yelps at its mistress and remained in its basket.

Miss Jensen took off her outdoor clothes and sat down in a corner and wept.

She wept every time she was alone since Mr Linde had said those words.

"You are interested in the school, vicar," she had said, "and so the parents send their children to the Free School."

"Let me tell you, Miss Jensen, why the parents send their children to the Free School: it is because Miss Sørensen knows her job well," the minister had said.

The innkeeper's wife was the only person to whom Miss Jensen had confided "the words":

"And what is an unmarried lady to do, Mrs Madsen?" she had said. "Tears are the only defence a woman has."

Miss Jensen sat weeping in her corner. Darkness began to fall, and finally she rose and went out into the kitchen.

She lit a small paraffin cooking stove and put some water on for tea. She laid a cloth across one corner of the kitchen table and arranged some bread and butter in front of the solitary plate.

But while she was doing this, she was lost in thought, pondering again on the vicar's words.

The pug had gone out with her and placed itself on a cushion in front of its empty dish.

Miss Jensen took the dish and filled it with white bread that had been softened in the warm water.

The pug had the dish placed before it and started eating the food almost without moving.

Miss Jensen had lit a solitary candle. She drank her tea with an open rye bread sandwich, using her knife to cut the bread into delicate little squares.

When she had drunk her tea, Miss Jensen went to bed. She carried the pug in her arms and put it down on the duvet at the foot of the bed. Then she fetched the school register and laid it on the table at the bedside.

She locked the door and looked in all the corners and under the bed by the light of her candle.

Then she undressed, combed out her plaits and hung them up on the mirror.

The pug was already asleep, snoring on the duvet.

Miss Jensen did not sleep well since Mr Linde had said those words.

Mrs Bai went back along the road towards the station. She opened the gate and went on to the platform. It was quite empty, so silent that you could hear the humming of the two telegraph wires.

With her hands on her lap, Mrs Bai sat down on the bench outside the door and looked out across the fields. Mrs Bai was much inclined to sit in this way wherever there was a chair or a bench or a flight of steps.

She looked out across the fields, the great stretches of ploughed land and the meadows beyond. The sky was clear and pale blue. There was nothing for the eyes to rest upon with ease, other than the chapel, you could see that with its stepped gables and the tower right over on the other side of the flat field.

Mrs Bai felt cold and got up. She went across to the garden hedge, looked in over it, opened the gate and entered. The garden was a triangular strip along the railway; there was a kitchen garden at the front, and behind this there was a lawn with some tall roses in front of the summer house beneath the elder bush.

She examined the roses; there were a few buds on them still. They had flowered faithfully all through the year.

But now they would soon have to be covered.

The leaves were falling already. But there was no protection for anything, of course.

Mrs Bai went out of the garden again and along the platform

into the little courtyard behind the wooden fencing. She called for the maid and told her she wanted to feed the pigeons.

She received the corn in an earthenware bowl and started to call the pigeons and scatter the corn out across the stones.

She was very fond of pigeons. She had been ever since she was a child.

There had been such a lot of them at home in the big merchant's house in the town. Oh how they used to flock around the dovecote just opposite the door leading into the workshop.

It was as though she could hear the cooing and murmuring merely by thinking of the courtyard at home.

That was the old house, for later, when her father died, they sold the old workshop and everything else, and moved away.

The pigeons flew down around Mrs Bai, picking at the corn.

"Marie," said Mrs Bai, "just come and see how bad-tempered the speckled one is."

Marie appeared in the kitchen door and discussed the pigeons. Mrs Bai emptied out the rest of the bowl. "Some of them are going to meet their fate when Bai's friends come to play *Hombre*."

She went up the steps. "It gets dark so early now," she said and went inside.

The living room was rather dark and felt warm as she came in from outside. Mrs Bai sat down at the piano and played a tune.

She never played except when it was growing dark, always the same three or four melodies, sentimental little things that she played languorously and slowly, all in the same manner so they all assumed the same quality.

As she sat there playing the piano in the dark sitting room, Mrs Bai almost always thought of her home. They had been a big family, and there had always been such a variety of things at home.

She was the youngest of them all. While her father was still alive, she was so small that she could hardly even reach her plate at dinner.

Her father would sit on the sofa in his shirt sleeves, and the children would stand around the table and help themselves.

"Straighten your backs, children," her father would say.

He himself would sit with his broad back slumped forward and his arms right across the table.

Her mother went to and fro, fetching and bringing.

The lads from the workshop all ate out in the kitchen, seated at the long table.

They giggled and argued so noisily that it could be heard through the door, and they suddenly made such a row that it sounded as though the house was about to collapse.

"What's all that din about?" her father shouted, banging the table in the living room.

They fell quite silent out in the kitchen. There was only a gentle scraping sound from one who was searching for something under the table after the kerfuffle.

"Dreadful crowd," said her father.

After lunch he slept for an hour on the sofa. He woke on the dot:

"Now I have given some serious thought to the country's best interests," he said, being given a cup of coffee before returning to the workshop.

Everything changed when her father died. Katinka was sent to the school along with Consul Lasson's children and the mayor's daughter Fanny.

And she was also invited to the consul's.

The other siblings were dispersed. She was left alone with her mother.

Those years were the best in Katinka's life, there in the little town where she knew everyone and everyone knew her. In the afternoons, she and her mother would sit in the drawing room, each at a window, her mother by the one with the "mirror"; Katinka would do French embroidery or read.

The sun fell in bright stripes through the flowers in the windows, out across the white floor.

Katinka read a great number of novels from the public library, novels about people of aristocratic birth, but she also read poems that she copied into an album.

"Tinka," said her mother. "Here comes Ida Levy. Oh, she's wearing her yellow hat."

Tinka looked up: "She's going for her music lesson," she said.

Ida Levy went past, and they looked at her and she nodded to them and asked with her fingers whether they were coming to meet the "half past nine".

"Oh, it's dreadful the way Ida Levy wears her heels down," said Tinka as she watched her.

"She gets that from her mother," said mother.

They go past, one by one, the land agent and the two lieutenants, the director and the doctor. And they wave to them, and upstairs they nod and exchange a few words about each of them.

They know where everyone is going and what they are going to do.

They know every costume and every flower on every hat. And every day they make the same comments about the same things.

Minna Helms passes and nods.

"Did you see Minna Helms?" says mother.

"Yes." And Katinka looks at her and screws up her eyes against the sun.

"She could do with a new coat," she says.

"Poor things, where are they going to get one from?" Her mother looks in the mirror: "Aye, it looks pretty worn," she says. "I think she could sew some new edging on it though. But it's probably as Mrs Noes says: Mrs Helms doesn't have much, and she isn't much bothered."

"If only that clerk of hers would pull himself together and do something about it," said Tinka.

Five o'clock came, and the young girls would call for each other to go for a walk, and arm in arm they would walk up and down the street, meeting and gathering in groups and laughing and chatting and going their way.

In the evenings, after tea, the mothers would come along as well to meet the half-past-nine train, and things were much quieter as they walked out along the station road.

"Katinka," said her mother, turning round – she was walking in front with Mrs Levy – "There's Mr Bai. So he must have the evening off."

Mr Bai passed by and greeted them. And Katinka nodded and blushed. For her friends were always teasing her about Mr Bai.

"So he is off to play skittles," said Mrs Levy.

On Sundays they went to church. Everyone wore their best clothes, and their singing resounded beneath the vaulted roof while the sun entered through the big chancel windows.

Thora Berg was such a naughty one to sit beside in church.

She sat there all the time the parson was in the pulpit, saying, "Well, my dear" and pinching her arm.

Aye, Thora Berg was quite a tomboy.

In the evening, soil and pebbles rained down against Tinka's windows.

And they heard noise and laughter all the way down the street.

"That's Thora going home from a party," said Tinka. "They've been at the mayor's."

Thora set off home along the street as if on a wild hunt, pursued by all the young gentlemen. The entire town was permitted to hear it when Thora Berg went home from a party.

Katinka liked Thora Berg most of all. She admired her and watched her attentively when they were together. At home, she would say "Thora said that" twenty times a day.

They did not actually spend a great deal of time in each other's company. But in the afternoons, when they were taking a walk, or out at the pavilion, where they had season tickets for the concerts the military band gave every other Wednesday, then they talked together. Tinka always became quite flushed when they met.

It was also at the pavilion she had first made the acquaintance of Bai. And on that very first evening he had danced most with her.

And when they were out skating, he always invited her to skate with him. It was as though they were flying, almost as though he was carrying her. And he also visited them at home.

All her friends teased her, and she always had him as a partner when they were playing party games or had guessing games. It was always Bai, and everyone laughed.

And mother was always talking about him at home.

Then came the engagement, and she always had someone to go with to church on Sundays; and in the winter, when there was a play on, to the theatre. And when Bai got his position there was that busy time with her trousseau and arranging the house and all that. Her friends helped her with all the names that had to be sewn and all the things that had to be hemmed.

They were summer days, and they all sat up in the summerhouse. The sewing machine whirred, making hems and fixing ends.

And they would tease her and laugh and suddenly bounce up and fly out into the garden, running around the lawn and making a noise and laughing, as wild as a group of foals.

Tinka was the quietest of them.

There was whispering with friends in every corner and sewing get-togethers at the Levys, where they sewed the rug that Tinka was to stand on as a bride before the altar, and there were the rehearsals for the hymns they were to sing in the choir.

Then came the day, and the wedding in the decorated church.It was quite full, even crowded. All the girls were up by the organ. Tinka nodded to them and thanked them and wept again. She had shed tears all the time as though a tap had been turned on.

And then they moved over here, to the silence.

At the beginning of her marriage, Tinka was frightened and always on edge, as though scared of being attacked.

There was so much she had not imagined, and Bai was so rough in many things that she simply suffered and put up with it, frightened and insecure as she was.

And she was also a stranger here and knew no one.

Then came a time when she became more acquiescent, more indolent and clingy, as was her nature.

She would sit with her crocheting in her husband's office, looking at him as he sat bent over his desk, her curly hair falling a little down over her forehead.

She would rise and go across to him and put her arm round

his neck, wanting to stand close to him, silent, to be close to him like this for a long time.

"I'm trying to write, you know, dear," Bai would say.

She would bend her neck down to his mouth and he would kiss it.

"Can I get on with my writing now," he would say, kissing her once more.

"You're always writing," she would say.

The years passed. Katinka adapted to life with the trains coming and going and the local people who went away and returned home; they brought news and they asked for news.

They established a social circle with such people as there were in the area. Mainly Bai's *Hombre* friends, accompanied every other time by their wives.

Then there was the dog and the pigeons and the garden. And Mrs Bai was not actually one of the most efficient of people. She rarely had time on her hands as she lingered for a long time over everything she did. Bai called her "I'll do it tomorrow".

There were no children.

When Katinka's mother died, they received her inheritance. As a couple on whom no calls were made they were well off and had everything in plenty.

Bai liked to eat well, and he ordered an abundance of good wine from Aalborg. He put on a little weight, living a life of some indolence and leaving his assistant to do most of the work. He only looked the "lieutenant" when he was outdoors.

He had a child up in town.

"What the hell," he said to Kiær, who was a bachelor, "I used to be in the cavalry and the girl was as sweet as a baby sparrow."

The girl went to Aalborg after the damage was done. The

child was fostered in the village.

And so time passed.

Katinka no longer read as she used to do as a girl. Books were just made up stories, after all.

Mrs Bai had in her escritoire a large cardboard box containing a host of withered flowers, ribbons, and bits and pieces of gauze adorned with gold lettering. They were her old mementoes from the *cotillions* in the club and the last dances in the pavilion balls.

She would often take all this out during the winter evenings and rearrange it and try to remember who had given her this and who that.

She worked it all out and she wrote the gentleman's name on the back of each cotillion card.

Bai sat at the table drinking his toddy.

"All that old rubbish," he said.

"Leave it alone, Bai," she would say, "Now I've just arranged it."

And she continued to write her gentlemen's names.

Occasionally, she would take out her album and read the verses she had copied into it in those days.

Her bridal veil and the withered myrtle wreath were kept in the top drawer below the silver cupboard in the escritoire.

She took that out as well and smoothed it down and put it together again.

And she would sit for half an hour over the open drawer and do nothing at all, as was her wont.

Occasionally she would simply smooth the veil out with her hands.

That bridal veil had started to turn quite yellow.

But time was passing as well. It was already ten years ago. Aye – she would soon be an old woman. She was thirty-two now.

The Bais were well liked in the district. Known as kind and hospitable people who were quick to put on the coffee pot when any of their acquaintances came to the station.

Bai was a hospitable man, and he had everything under control in the station despite his not being particular about his dress.

His wife was rather quiet, but it was always good to see her kind face. She looked just like a young girl when sitting among the other ladies at the big *Hombre* evenings.

"But they ought to have a couple of children," said Mrs Linde as she walked home with the vicar from the Bais."Well-to-do people, they can afford it. It is a great pity that they should be there on their own."

"God gives life according to His will, my dear," said the vicar.

"Yes, God's will be done," said his wife.

The vicar and his wife had had ten children.

God had taken seven of them into His care when small. The old vicar remembered the seven every time there were children to be buried in the parish.

Mrs Bai had stopped playing the piano. She sat thinking that she really ought to get up and light the lamp. But then she called the maid and told her to light it and remained seated.

Marie came in with the lamp. She put a cloth on the table and laid it for tea.

"What time is it?" asked Mrs Bai.

"The eight o'clock train is signalled," said Marie.

"I hadn't heard that."

Mrs Bai put on a coat and went out: "Is the train here?" she asked at the office.

"It'll be here in a moment," said Bai. He was standing by the telegraph desk.

"Is there a telegram?"

"Yes."

"Who for?"

"Oh, up in town."

"That means Ane will have to be off."

Mrs Bai went out onto the platform. She was so fond of seeing the trains come and go in the dark.

The sound, at first far away, and then the rumbling as the train went over the bridge across the river and the great light at the head of it and finally the heavy swaying bulk emerging from the dark. It twisted its way forward and turned into distinct carriages that drew to a halt before her with guards, lighted post wagons and compartments.

Then, when it had gone again and the rumbling had died away, all was silent, as though twice as quiet.

The porter turned out the lights, first the one on the platform and then the one above the door.

There was no light apart from what came through the two windows, two narrow bridges of light in the vast darkness.

Mrs Bai went indoors.

They had a cup of tea, and then Bai read the papers, accompanying them with a toddy or two. He only read the government press. He personally took the *Nationaltidende* and then he read Kiær's *Dagblad*, which he took out of the mail bag.

He thumped the table, making the toddy glass chink when the opposition was given "a real kick in the teeth". And he would occasionally read the odd sentence aloud and laugh.

Mrs Bai listened and said nothing; she was not interested in politics. Besides that, she was going through a period of feeling terribly sleepy in the evenings.

"I suppose it's about time," said Bai.

He rose and lit a lantern. He did his round to make sure that everything was shut and the track was in order for the night train.

"You can go to bed, Marie," said Mrs Bai in the direction of the kitchen. She woke Marie, who was sitting asleep on the wooden chair.

"Good night, ma'am," she said drowsily.

"Good night."

Mrs Bai moved the flowers in the living room away from the window ledge and put them down on the floor, where they spent the night standing in a row.

Bai returned.

"It's getting cold at night," he said.

"I was thinking of that for the roses. I was seeing to them today."

"Aye," he said, "they'll have to be covered over now."

Bai started to undress in the bedroom. The door was open.

He was very fond of going to and fro in the evening. From the bedroom to the sitting room in a state of near undress.

"She does lumber about," he said. Marie was treading hard on the floor up in the attic.

Mrs Bai placed white sheets on the furniture and locked the office door.

"Can I put the light out?" she said.

And she extinguished the lamp.

She went into the bedroom, sat down before the mirror and loosened her hair.

Bai, in his underpants, asked for a pair of scissors.

"You're losing a hell of a lot of weight," he said.

Katinka pulled the dressing gown around her.

Bai got into bed and lay there talking. She replied as always in her own quiet way. There was always a quite brief pause before the words came out.

They had been silent for a while.

"Hmm, quite a nice person, don't you think?"

"Yes, judging by his looks."

"What did Agnes Linde say?"

"She said he looked quite nice, too."

"Hmm, the things that girl says!"

"And God knows what kind of a hand he plays at *Hombre*."

It was not long before Bai was asleep.

When he was asleep, Bai breathed heavily through his nose.

Mrs Bai was used to that now.

She remained sitting in front of the mirror. She took off her dressing gown and looked at her neck.

Yes, she had really become very thin.

It was since she had had that cough in the spring.

Mrs Bai put out the lights and lay down in bed beside Mr Bai.

II

The short days had come now.

Pouring rain and such tedious slush. But always a grey sky and always wet. Even Miss Jensen's nicest pupils wore clogs as they came to school across the fields.

At the station, the platform was a lake. The last little leaves from the garden hedge were floating in it. The trains arrived dripping wet; the guards dashed back and forth wrapped in wet cloaks. Wee Bentzen ran around carrying the postbags beneath his umbrella.

Kiær's grain trucks were covered with tarpaulin sheets, and the drivers sat there in rain capes.

Huus, the new bailiff, drove the first wagon to the station himself. There was plenty to see to with freight and clearance.

"Kiær's folk are here," said Bai to his wife.

Huus was in the habit of taking off his raincoat for half an hour and having a cup of coffee with the Bais.

While Mrs Bai went to and fro laying the table for coffee, Huus and the farm workers went back and forth on the platform, loading the sacks onto the goods wagons. Katinka saw them running past the windows. They looked so huge in their oilskins.

Marie, the maid, had a crush on Huus and went on about him all the time while she was at work.

She never tired of talking of his fine qualities. And she

34

always ended with: "And what a voice he's got."

It was a soft, honest voice, and no one knew why Marie should have fallen for it.

When Huus had finished outside, they went in for coffee. It was warm and comfortable, and there was the scent of a couple of potted plants still flowering on the window ledge.

Aye, that's what I always say," said Huus, rubbing his hands, "It's nice and cosy in Mrs Bai's sitting room."

And Huus brought a feeling of cosiness with him, too. There was a quiet sense of contentment about him; he said very little, and he rarely "told" anything. But he joined so easily in the everyday gossip, cheerful, always in a good mood. And it felt good simply to have him there.

A goods train arrived just at that moment, and Bai had to go out on the platform to attend to it.

It made no difference when he went and the other two were left alone. They chatted a little or sat quietly. She went across to the window and laughed at Bai as he rushed about in the rain out there.

Huus saw to Katinka's flowers and gave her advice as to how to look after them. Katinka went across to him, and they tended them together. He knew every single one of them, whether it was growing or whether it was dormant, and he knew what to do with them.

Huus was interested in all small things of this kind, in the pigeons and the new strawberry patch that had been planted during the autumn.

Katinka asked his advice, and they went around looking at this and looking at that.

Bai had never been interested in that kind of thing. But with Huus it was as though there was always something new to learn, something to be asked about and something to arrange.

In that way they always had plenty to talk about, quietly and slowly, as was the manner with both of them.

Indeed, there was almost always something waiting for Huus – even if he came virtually every day, as he did just at this time when Rugaard Farm was selling its grain.

Miss Ida Abel also often had a reason for going to the station. She would struggle down the road with a letter she wanted to catch the midday post.

"Heaven help us, what dreadful weather, lieutenant."

"A cup of coffee, miss? A little internal moisture to help you cope. Huus is inside with my wife."

"Are the folk from Rugaard here?"

"Yes, they've come with some grain."

Ida had had no idea they were there.

From the elevated ground at the corner of the farm, the "chicks" could keep an eye on the entire area.

Ida spent her mornings there.

She started to take the curlers out of her hair.

"Where are you going?"

Louise had toothache and was countering it with a spice bag.

"To the station with a letter."

"Mother," whined Louise, "now Ida's off again. Hmm, if you think you'll get anywhere down there…"

"What has it to do with you?" Ida slammed the bedroom door in the face of her fellow chick.

"Good lord, do you really want to make a fool of yourself? But you can put your own boots on. I'm telling you that, Ida."

"Mother, tell Ida to put her own boots on, she always puts mine on to go to the station."

"Pooh," says Ida, who had now finished with the curling tongs.

"And my gloves – for heaven's sake!" Louise snatches a

pair of gloves out of Ida's hands. And once more a couple of doors are slammed.

"What was all that about, children?" says Mrs Abel. She enters from the kitchen with wet hands. She has been peeling potatoes.

"Ida's pinching my clothes." Louise is weeping with fury.

Mrs Abel, quietly tidies up after her younger daughter and returns to her potatoes.

"My dear Mrs Bai," says Ida, "I will not come inside. Good day, Mr Huus, I look so awful… I'm just looking in. Good day."

Miss Abel came in. She had a low-cut dress beneath her rain cape.

"It's when Christmas is approaching there is such a dreadful lot to be done. Oh, would you excuse me, Mr Huus, if I push past you and join you on the sofa. It's nice to sit down," she said.

But she did not sit there for long. There were too many things she had to admire. Miss Ida Abel was so full of youthful enthusiasm.

"Oh what a sweet little rug!"

"Oh, Mr Huus, do you mind?" She had to get past him again.

She felt the rug.

"Mother always says I flutter all over the place," said Ida.

Mrs Abel sometimes called her daughters her little doves, but the name failed to catch on. There was something about Louise that absolutely excluded the concept of a dove.

And the "chicks" continued to be the term used.

After Miss Abel's arrival, it was not long before Mr Huus took his leave.

There was not room for so many in a sitting room when Miss Ida was there, he said.

Christmas was approaching.

Huus went to Randers on business once a week. He always had some errand to do for Mrs Bai. Bai must not be told. The two of them would whisper about it for a long time in the sitting room when Huus had come back on the train.

Katinka thought it must have been many years since she had looked forward to Christmas as much as she did this year.

The weather helped as well.

There was a light, tingling frost and snow on the ground.

When Huus had been in Randers he stayed for tea at the station. He came with the eight o'clock train. Mrs Bai was often still sitting in the dark.

"Will you play something for me?" he said.

"Oh, I only know a few pieces."

"But if I would like to hear them?" He sat on a chair in a corner beside the sofa.

Katinka played her five pieces; they all resembled each other. She would otherwise never think of playing for anyone. But Huus sat so quietly over in his corner that his presence was simply not noticed. And besides, he had no musical sense whatever.

When she had played, they would sit for a time without saying anything until Marie came in with the lamp and the tea things.

After tea, Bai took Huus with him into the office.

"Men must occasionally be left on their own as well," he said.

When he and Huus were alone, Bai told all sorts of stories about women.

He had also figured in them once, when they were all in the training school.

"And Copenhagen had its women in those days. Oh well. Things have gone downhill since."

"They say they all go to Russia now. All right, that might well be, I suppose."

"But things have gone downhill."

"If you'd known Kamilla – Kamilla Andersen – fine girl – wonderful girl. She came to a sad end – she damn well went and threw herself out of a window."

"Ambitious girl." Bai winked. Huus pretended he understood Kamilla's ambition.

"Very ambitious girl… Knew her well. Brilliant."

Bai talked all the time. Huus smoked his cigar and did not look particularly interested.

"And," said Bai, "I ask the young people, you know, in the summer holidays, in the parsonage gardens, 'What sort of women do you get nowadays?' I ask them. Are they any good?"

"Little girls, my friend. Little girls."

"Aye, they say they go to Russia, and that might well be, damn it."

Huus expressed no opinion as to where they went. He looked at the clock.

"It's getting on," he said.

"Oh, I don't know."

But Huus had to go. The walk would take him three quarters of an hour after all.

They went in to join Mrs Bai in the sitting room.

"Should we not walk some of the way with Huus?" she said. "The weather is so beautiful."

"Good idea, damn it. Give us a bit of exercise."

They went with him.

Katinka took Bai's arm. She had Huus on the other side. The snow creaked beneath their feet as they walked along the road.

"What a lot of stars there are this year," said Katinka.

"Yes, a lot more than last year, Tik." Bai was always animated when he had been in his own room.

"Yes, I think there are," said Katinka.

"It's curious weather," said Huus.

"Yes," this came from Bai: "All this cold before Christmas."

"And it is going to last over New Year."

"Do you think so?"

Then they fell silent, and when they spoke again it was more or less a repeat of the same conversation.

At the turn of the road, the Bais said good night.

Mrs Bai hummed a tune as she walked along. When they reached home, she remained in the doorway while Bai fetched the lantern and went across to see to the track for the night train.

He came back. "Well," he said.

Katinka breathed out in the air, slowly.

"I do so like this cold weather," she said, drawing her hand through her own breath as it rose in the air.

They went inside.

Bai lay in bed, smoking a cigar butt. Then he said,

"Aye, Huus is a damn nice chap but he's a dry old stick."

Mrs Bai was sitting in front of the looking glass. She laughed.

But Bai told Kiær in confidence that he didn't believe Huus knew a damn thing about women. "I try to bring him out a bit, you know, in the evenings when he's down at our house, but by Gad I don't think he knows much about women."

"Well, old chap," said Kiær, and they slapped each other's shoulders and laughed happily. "We can't all be connoisseurs, you know."

"No – fortunately. And as for Huus, I'm damn sure he isn't."

They were called in for coffee.

The last days before Christmas were a busy time at the station. There were so many things to be fetched and dispatched. No one wanted to wait for the postman.

The Misses Abel sent small cards with best wishes and enquired about parcels.

Miss Jensen brought a box of cigars with a whole stick of sealing wax spread decoratively on the string around it

"My own handiwork, Mrs Bai," said Miss Jensen. The handiwork was for her sister.

Mrs Bai said, "Mrs Abel was at Randers yesterday, you know."

"The interest on her annuity was due for payment yesterday," said Miss Jensen tartly.

"She was so laden with parcels when she came home."

"I can well believe that."

"I suppose you are going to the Abels for Christmas Eve?"

"No. We live next door, Mrs Bai, but the Abels always have plenty to do thinking of themselves. I always used to go to the Lindes, in the parsonage. No, the Abels," said Miss Jensen, "It's not everyone who is one's..."

Mrs Bai asked Miss Jensen if she would perhaps make do with them.

She brought herself to tell Bai when he came home from the tracks that evening.

"Mathias," she said, she called him Mathias when about

to make some dubious communication, "I have had to invite little Miss Jensen here for Christmas Eve. She can't go to the Lindes."

"That's all right as far as I'm concerned." Bai hated "the little wig stand" as he called her. "You are welcome to your collection of waifs and strays."

Bai walked to and fro.

"Isn't she going to the Abels?" he said.

"That's just the problem, they haven't invited her, Mathias."

"Oh, that was probably wise of them, damn it," said Bai, throwing his boots off. "Oh well, if it makes you happy."

Mrs Bai was pleased she had managed to say it.

Miss Jensen came at half past five, bringing with her a splint basket and the pug.

She apologized for Bel-Ami.

"He's at the Abels otherwise – I always leave him with the Abels. But this evening, you see, I didn't want... but he'll not do any harm... he's a very quiet animal."

Bel-Ami was placed on a rug in the bedroom. And there he stayed. He suffered from sleeping sickness and was no trouble apart from the fact that he snored.

"He is a good sleeper," said Miss Jensen, taking cuffs and a collar out of the splint basket.

Bel-Ami was only difficult when he was to go home. He had certainly lost all taste for exercise.

At every tenth step he would stand still and howl with his tail between his legs.

When no one was looking, Miss Jensen would pick him up and carry him.

They dined at six o'clock. The "tree" stood in a corner. Wee Bentzen had his hair done in a quiff and was wearing his confirmation suit.

He ate like a horse.

Bai filled the glasses and chinked with Miss Jensen and Wee Bentzen .

"Well, cheers, Miss Jensen."

"Cheers, Bentzen my boy. It's only Christmas once a year," he said. He poured more into the boy's glass.

Wee Bentzen blushed and his complexion was that of a lobster.

"We're drinking like they did in heathen times," said Miss Jensen.

The door was open to the office. The telegraph ticked ceaselessly.

Colleagues were telegraphing Christmas wishes to each other. Bai went back and forth to answer them.

"Give them my best wishes," said Katinka.

"Greetings from Mundstrup," said Bai from the apparatus.

"Yes," said Miss Jensen, "that is what I say to my pupils: I often tell them that our age has overcome the bounds of space."

When the time came for cakes Miss Jensen became quite lively. Like a child, she nodded to herself in the mirror and said, "Cheers".

Miss Jensen was wearing a new chignon that she had treated herself to for Christmas. Her hair was now in three different shades.

Bit by bit, Miss Jensen became rather happy.

After the meal, while the candles were being lit on the tree, Bentzen tried to play leapfrog with Marie the maid out in the kitchen.

Katinka went quietly around and took her time in lighting the candles. She probably also wanted to be on her own for a while.

"I wonder whether Huus has received our parcel," she said.

She was standing on a chair, using a wax candle to do the lighting.

At the last moment she took a muslin scarf from her table, it was one she had received from a sister, and put it among Miss Jensen's presents. There were so few in her place; she was sharing the sofa with Wee Bentzen.

Katinka opened the door to the office, and they came in to see the tree.

They went around and looked at their presents, saying thank you for them and looking slightly embarrassed. Miss Jensen took out some small tissue paper packages from the splint basket and distributed them.

Marie the maid came in wearing a white apron. She went around with her own presents in her arms and felt the various objects scattered round about.

The eight o'clock train was dispatched, and they were again in the sitting room. The candles on the tree were still burning over in the corner.

It was very warm and stuffy in there because of the candles on the tree.

Bai made a show of fighting with sleep and said, "One is soon check-mated by all this festivity, Miss Jensen. All this Christmas jollification is pretty tiring."

They were all sleepy and were eying the clock. The two ladies insisted on talking about the presents again and saying how good the work on them was.

"I think I'll go and reflect a little on the state of the world," said Bai. He escaped into the office. Wee Bentzen sat sleeping in a chair beneath the pipe rack.

The two ladies were left alone. They sat in a corner near the piano, in front of the tree, and were very sleepy.

They had been dozing for a time and suddenly jumped up

in alarm at the sound of crackling in the tree. A branch had caught fire.

"It won't burn much longer now," said Katinka as she put out the fire.

The candles started to burn out one by one, and the tree grew dark. They sat there, quite awake again, looking at the darkening tree, there were just a couple of candles left burning low.

They were both overcome by the same quiet sense of melancholy as they looked at these last little candles. It was as though they only served to emphasize the dark, dead tree.

Miss Jensen started to speak. Katinka scarcely heard at first what it was she was saying, deeply absorbed in her own thoughts about the family at home and about Huus.

Katinka did not know why she had been thinking so much about Huus throughout the evening. He had been in her thoughts all the time.

All the time.

She nodded to Miss Jensen and pretended she was listening.

Miss Jensen was talking about her youth and suddenly plunged into telling the story of her love. She was already well into her account when Katinka became aware of it and she was surprised that Miss Jensen came to talk about it now and to her.

It was quite a simple story about unrequited love. She had believed it was her who was the focus of affection, and then it turned out to be her friend.

Miss Jensen spoke quietly, all the time in the same hushed voice. She had her handkerchief out and occasionally she would sniff a little and dab her cheeks with it.

Katinka gradually became rather moved. Then she thought of how this wrinkled little person would have looked as a young woman. Perhaps after all she had had a neat little figure.

And there she sat now, deserted and alone.

Katinka was quite affected, and she took Miss Jensen's hands and gently patted them.

The caresses made the old woman weep still more. Katinka continued to pat her hands.

The last stumps of candle burned down, and the Christmas tree stood there quite dark.

"And a maiden lady has to get through life," said Miss Jensen, "Whatever traps are put before her."

Miss Jensen was back on the subject of the parson and his "words".

Katinka released Miss Jensen's hand. She felt it had grown quite cold and unpleasant around the tree now the candles had died.

Bai opened the door to the brightly lit office. A messenger had arrived on horseback bringing a parcel from Huus.

"Lanterns, Marie," shouted Katinka, running into the office with the parcel.

It was a very finely woven shawl with gold threads in it, a big one that could be folded tight and almost into nothing.

Katinka remained standing there with the shawl. She was so pleased with it. She had had one quite similar to this, and a couple of weeks ago she had had an accident and burnt it.

But this one was much more splendid.

And she continued to stand there holding the shawl.

Bai was in a merry mood again. He had had a sleep and got over the dinner, and they all had some real rum in their tea.

Wee Bentzen became so high spirited that he ran over to his room and fetched some poems he had written down on a variety of paper scraps, the backs of old price lists and bills.

He read aloud so that Bai had to slap his thighs and roar

with laughter. Katinka sat smiling, wrapped in Huus' splendid shawl.

Miss Jensen finally played a Tyrolean waltz, and Wee Bentzen rushed into the kitchen, just a little embarrassed, and waltzed around so eagerly with Marie that she gave a little shriek.

They all had to help to wake Bel-Ami up again when Miss Jensen was to leave; he simply refused to leave his rug. Bai trod on its stub of a tail when Miss Jensen turned away.

Wee Bentzen was to take her home, but Miss Jensen, who was as scared as could be of the dark, insisted on going alone.

Miss Jensen refused to carry her Bel-Ami when anyone was watching.

They all went with her as far as the platform gate and shouted "Happy Christmas", "Happy Christmas" over the hedge.

Bel-Ami set up a howl on the snow-covered road. He refused to move.

When Miss Jensen was sure they had all gone inside, she bent down and took Bel-Ami up in her arms.

Miss Jensen was wrapped up like an Eskimo woman as she walked home that Christmas night.

Katinka opened the windows to the living room, letting in the piercing cold air.

"Hmm, that little fraud knows how to put it on," said Bai. He felt a measure of benevolent pleasure at having had little Miss Jensen there this evening.

"The poor little thing," said Katinka. She remained at the window, looking out across the white field into the night.

"No one would think you were complaining of a cough," said Bai. He closed the door to the bedroom.

Bentzen went over the platform to his room.

"She carried the pug," he said. He had hidden behind the

hedge to see this event. "Happy Christmas, Madam."

"Happy Christmas, Bentzen ."

A couple of doors were closed, and then all was quite silent.

Just occasionally there was a fine humming sound in the telegraph wires.

Katinka was outside feeding the pigeons before going to church. The air was clear and there was no sign of a breeze, and the bells could be heard from the other side of the woods. All around in the white fields, the farmers could be seen trudging to church in single file along paths that had been cleared of snow.

They waited together outside the church, wishing each other a Happy Christmas. The women touched the tips of each other's gloves and spoke in whispers.

Then they stood in silence and looked at each other until someone else joined the group.

The Bais were rather late and the church was full. Katinka nodded "Happy Christmas" to Huus, who was standing close to the door, and went up to her place.

She shared a pew with the Abels, just behind the minister's family.

The Abel chicks were hidden in veils and fantastic lacework.

Mrs Linde had eyes in the back of her head on the major offertory days. She dressed herself and her daughter suitably on the days when there was a collection for the clergy.

Her daughter never went to church on the days when "the plate was passed round".

They sang the old Christmas hymns, and bit by bit they all joined in, big and small. The vaulting was filled with an ample happy sound. The wintry sun shone in through the windows on to the white walls. Old Linde preached on the shepherds in the fields and the people for whom a Saviour was born this day, speaking in quiet, simple words so that it was as though the peace of simplicity descended on his church.

Katinka fell into a Christmas mood as the long procession to make the offerings slowly moved around the altar. The men walked stiffly, tramping heavily on the tiles and returned to their seats with completely expressionless faces.

The women sat shuffling a little, embarrassed and red-faced, their eyes stiffly directed towards the folded cloth.

Mrs Linde had her eyes on people's hands at the altar.

Mrs Linde had been a parson's wife for thirty-five years and had sat through countless offertory days. She could see from their hands what sort of contribution everyone was making.

Hands moved differently on coming out of pockets according to whether they were giving a small or a larger amount.

Mrs Linde estimated the offerings to be average this year.

The Bais met Huus outside the church. People were catching their breath out in the fresh air, and once more everyone wished everyone else a happy Christmas.

The minister came with the offertory money tied up in a handkerchief and everyone greeted him and curtseyed. "Well, Miss Jensen, I suppose we must all wish each other a happy Christmas," said the "old minister".

Katinka went out through the churchyard gate together with Huus. Bai stayed behind for a while with Kiær, so the two of them walked down the road alone together.

The sun was shining on the glistening fields; farms here and there had their flag flying high up on the flagpoles.

Churchgoers were drifting off home here and there together.

Katinka could still hear the hymns ringing in her ears, and she felt it all as a happy, solemn occasion.

"Christmas is a nice time," she said.

"Yes," he replied, putting all his conviction into that one word, "yes".

"And he also preached quite well," he added shortly afterwards.

"Yes," said Katinka, "it was a really nice sermon."

They walked on a little.

"But, you know, I haven't thanked you for the shawl," Katinka said.

"Don't mention it."

"But yes, of course… I was so delighted. I had one almost like it and had managed to burn it badly."

"Yes, I know… You were wearing it the day I arrived."

Katinka was on the point of saying, "How did you notice that?" But she refrained. Nor did she know why she suddenly blushed and for the first time noted that they were walking along without saying anything and tried to find something with which to break the silence.

They came down to the woods, and the bell from the chapel of ease rang out. It was as though the bells simply refused to stop ringing today.

"You will come in, won't you," said Katinka. "That will let Christmas into the house."

They stood on the platform and listened to the bells while waiting for Bai.

Huus spent the rest of the day there.

When Bai sat down at a table resplendent with its damask cloth and an array of glass plates, he said, "Aye, it's nice to have your family round you."

Wee Bentzen shouted, "Yes, it is," and laughed delightedly.

Huus said nothing. As Katinka said, he simply sat there and looked so content.

And throughout the day it was as though the house was suffused with a quiet happiness.

That evening, they played whist. Wee Bentzen was the fourth hand.

In the parsonage, they counted the offertory money. Mrs Linde was disappointed. The offerings were far less than average.

"What is the reason for it, Linde?" she asked.

The minister sat looking pensively at the large number of small coins.

"The reason for it? These people think we can live like the lilies of the field."

Mrs Linde paused for a moment and then for the last time counted the number of krone coins.

"With a family," concluded Mrs Linde.

"Well, my dear," said old Linde, "let us at least be grateful for the fact that the price of corn has risen, that after all is what the tithes are based on."

The parson's daughter and Mr Andersen the curate were having fun overturning the furniture in the hall: they were playing indoor croquet.

"I'm keeping out of mother's way," said Miss Agnes. "All her less noble qualities are in turmoil on the big offertory days."

Christmas came and went.

Katinka thought that she could not recall having such a lovely, homely Christmas like this for a long time, not since she was at home. Not that anything special happened, nothing more than usual; they visited the Lindes together with Huus and a couple of other people, and Miss Linde and the curate came to them one evening with Kiær and Huus. The Misses

Abel were there for the afternoon train and they were also invited inside. And after the eight o'clock train they danced in the waiting room and sang a few songs as well.

There was nothing special. But it was as though everything had gone off so happily.

The only person to upset things a little was Huus. He had frequently of late just sat dozing.

"Huus," said Katinka. "Are you asleep?"

Huus started as he sat there.

Bai was captured by the general sense of contentment in the house.

"I must say the weather makes a hell of a lot of difference," he said, standing on the platform after seeing the afternoon train off; "I'm feeling fine at the moment – damned fine, amazingly fine."

And during these days their entire marriage seemed as if it had been moved years back in time. Not in any insistent or excited manner, but in a way that was both intimate and cheerful.

It was approaching midnight on New Year's Eve. The Bais were up to let in the New Year.

A great banging was heard on the paling.

"What the hell," said Bai. It gave a shock to both him and Bentzen, who were playing cards, "There was no need for Peter to make such a din."

Someone knocked on the window, and Huus' voice could be heard shouting, "Happy New Year."

"What the Devil – is it Huus?" said Bai, getting up.

"That was my first thought," said Katinka. The din had given her palpitations.

Bai went out and opened up. Huus was in a sleigh.

"Good heavens," said Bai. "Won't you come in and have

a drink."

"Good evening, Huus," Katinka came into the doorway. "We're having a drink to welcome the New Year."

They tethered the horse in the storehouse, and Katinka gave it some bread.

They drank to the New Year and decided they would stay up until the night train went by. That would be at two o'clock.

"Play us a tune, Tik," said Bai.

Katinka played a polka, and Bai hummed along with her.

"Aye," he said, "I was a good dancer in my day, wasn't I Tik?" He tickled her neck.

They went out onto the platform. The sky was dark for the first time for ages.

"There's more snow on the way," said Bai. He took a little loose snow and rubbed it in Wee Bentzen's face. The result was a momentary general scuffle.

"There he is," said Bai. They could hear the distant rumble of the train.

"It's damned dark tonight, though," said Bai.

The noise came closer. Now the engine was rumbling across the bridge. The tiny light came closer and grew bigger; then the engine emerged suddenly from the darkness like some huge, bright-eyed beast.

And they all four stood still while it quickly rattled past. Steam rose from the track while lights from the coaches reflected across the snow.

It rattled away, off into the darkness.

"Hmm," said Katinka. "That's the way we greet the New Year." They had stood silent for a time.

She leant against her husband and stroked her hair against his cheek.

Bai was also moved by the situation. He bent down and

kissed her.

The train could be heard rumbling far away. They all turned round and went inside.

Huus was hard on the horse as he drove home in the sleigh. He lashed it cruelly and swore at it for good measure.

It was dark and a gale was approaching.

Katinka could not sleep. She woke Bai.

"Bai," she said.

"What is it?" Bai turned over.

"It's dreadful weather…"

"Well, we're not at sea, are we," said Bai, half asleep.

"But it's drifting so," said Katinka. "Do you think Huus has got home by now, Bai?"

"Oh, good Lord…"

Bai went back to sleep.

But Katinka did not sleep. She was worried about Huus on his way home in that weather. It was so dark and when all was said and done, he was new to the area.

How strange it was to think that it was only thirteen months since Huus had arrived.

Katinka wondered whether he really was home by now. She listened to the wind again; it was growing stronger. And he had been sad this evening, just sitting there – she knew him – and looking dejected. There must be something wrong.

There had been something wrong with him recently.

But would he have reached home by now? The weather was getting worse.

Katinka dropped off and fell asleep beside her husband.

On the second of January there was a party at the parsonage.

Half the local populace arrived, and people stood chatting in all the rooms and even out in the hall. It was always the case that people found a lot to talk about when they came to the parsonage.

The Abel family only arrived after the charades had started. They always came late.

"We didn't notice the time," said Mrs Abel. "We simply cannot tear ourselves away from the nest."

When the Misses Abel were to go out, they went around all afternoon wearing dressing gowns and quarrelling. Mrs Abel had to dress at the last moment and always looked as though a gale had swept over her.

They played charades, ensuring that there was not a stitch left untouched in the parsonage wardrobe.

Miss Agnes played the part of a fat man in the cottager's trousers and then a Greenlander with Katinka as the Greenlander's wife.

"Lovely lady," she said. "There is nothing fuddy-duddy about you."

They danced the *pingasut* until Katinka was quite dizzy. Mrs Bai was so happy that she was almost giddy.

Ida was in charge of the next bit. It was mainly something about a harem or a large spa. Whatever it was, the younger daughter Ida was embraced and hugged by a gaunt, fair-haired second lieutenant.

The older people gathered in the doorways to watch. Outside the hall windows in the garden stood the farmhand and the lads, all laughing at the clever Miss Agnes.

Old Mr Linde went back and forth:

"They are having fun, they are enjoying themselves," he said as he mingled with the older guests.

Mrs Abel was watching the parson; she was sitting beside the miller's wife:

"Yes, it's all very lively."

"Yes," said the miller's wife. "A very lively parsonage." Her voice was a little severe in the way she said "parson".

Her Helene stood beside her mother. She preferred not to take part in the games.

The miller had built a new house and the family were on their way up. They gave two parties a year, at which people sat in circles and stared at the new furniture. Everything continued to be new.

All the furniture was adorned with bits and pieces sewn and stitched by Miss Helene.

In everyday life, the family lived in one room in "the old wing". Once a week they lit fires in the main building so that the furniture should not suffer.

Miss Helene was an only child. She had been brought up by Miss Jensen with special emphasis on being taught foreign languages. She was the most elegant lady in the district and had a clear predilection for gold jewelry. Whatever her dress, she always wore grey felt shoes and white cotton stockings when she was indoors.

In company, she was easily upset and took up a position beside her mother with an acerbic expression on her face.

"Yes," says Mrs Abel, "my chicks sometimes find it a little on the lively side."

"Mother," says Ida, "give me your handkerchief."

"I need it now." And Ida almost snatches it off the widow.

Ida is to play a part wearing a nightcap and has discovered that her own handkerchief is rather less than perfect.

"They put all their hearts into the game," said Mrs Abel to the miller's wife.

The charades are finished, and they have a quick game of blind man's buff before the meal. There is such a din in the hall and a rushing about sufficient to make the old stove rattle.

"The stove," they shriek, "the stove."

"Be careful, be careful."

Ida is so worn out that she is ready to drop. Her heart is beating so she is unable to catch her breath: "Just feel," she says, placing the lieutenant's hand on her breast, "how my heart is beating."

Katinka is "it" and is turned around until she can scarcely stand.

"Oh, just watch the lovely lady," shouts Miss Agnes.

"Watch out, watch out."

Katinka catches Huus.

"Who is it?"

Huus bends down, and Katinka feels his hair: "It's Huus," she shouts. Old Reverend Linde claps his hands and announces that dinner is ready.

"Huus," says Katinka, "what's wrong? There's something the matter with you."

"What makes you think that?"

"You have not been happy recently, not like you used to be."

"There is nothing wrong, Mrs Bai."

"While I," said Katinka, "am just so happy."

"Yes," said Huus, "I can see that."

Bai came from the games table: "Good Lord, what a mess you look."

Katinka laughed: "Yes, we've been doing a Greenlandic dance." She went to a table accompanied by Huus.

Bai snatches Ida from the lieutenant, who follows together with the schoolteacher's son.

"Hansen," says the lieutenant, "who is that girl?"

"Oh, her mother's that lopsided woman over there with the minister; she's been pensioned off and given a house to live in up on the farm."

"Hell of a girl," says the lieutenant. "And what a figure she's got."

They are all seated; the minister sits at the top of the table. During the meal he proposes two toasts: "to absent friends" and "to the good spirit among those here present". People have drunk these very same toasts throughout his seventeen years in the parsonage.

Finally there is an almond cake and crackers. The minister pulls a cracker with Miss Jensen.

The lieutenant has managed to wedge a chair in behind Ida. It is such a tight squeeze that she almost has to sit on his lap.

Talking is out of the question as they laugh and pull crackers and read the mottos out loud.

"Aye," says old Linde, "that is youth."

"It's us, Huus," says Katinka, holding out a cracker.

Huus takes it. "You got the motto," says Katinka.

Huus reads the tiny slip of paper: "Nonsense," he says and tears it in two.

"But Huus, what did it say?"

"Every confectioner's assistant writes about love," says Ida across the table.

"Miss Ida," said the lieutenant, "shall we too?"

Ida turns and makes eyes at the lieutenant: "Good Lord, how inappropriate," she shouts. She receives a motto about kissing, which the lieutenant reads out with his little moustache close up to her cheek.

The chairs are moved a little further from the table, and the ladies wave their napkins. The young folk are flushed with heat and the milk punch that is being served from large grey jugs.

A pasty-faced little student calls for people to drink to "the Reverend Linde's patriarchal home", and everyone rises and shouts hurrah. The little student chinks glasses privately with the parson.

"You little red rascal," says old Linde, "Are you drinking to me?"

"One has to respect certain people," says the pasty-faced little man.

"Aye, aye," says old Linde. "Aye, youth must have something to fight for, you see madam."

Mrs Abel is preoccupied with her younger daughter Ida. Ida is so vivacious. She is almost lying in the lieutenant's arms.

"Yes, your reverence," she says.

"My dear Ida," (the dear daughter pays no attention) "Ida, drink a glass with your mamma," says Mrs Abel.

"Good health," says Ida. "Lieutenant Nielsen," she hands him his glass, "drink with mother."

Mrs Abel smiles, "Oh dear, what ideas my little Ida has."

The pasty-faced little man wants to know whether Miss Helene has read Schandorph.

Miss Helene is reading one of his books at present from the lending library.

"Schandorph has his merits – but he lacks the larger perspective." The little student feels obliged to say that Gjellerup is his *writer*.

Miss Helene cannot recall whether Mr. Gjellerup's books are available from the lending library.

"I call that entire movement the most genuine fruit of our mighty critic Brandes… intellectual freedom," continued the little student.

"Brandes, he's that Jew, isn't he?" says Miss Helene. That is all the 'intellectual freedom' that is left in the mill.

The student launches into the subject of the mighty Darwin.

Bai has said something to make Miss Jensen blush.

"You are so dreadful," says Little Miss Jensen and raps his knuckles.

"But Huus," says Katinka, "you have to take life as it is, and…"

"And?"

"And it is really so lovely."

"Lieutenant," shouts Miss Ida, "you are horrible."

Old Reverend Linde sits at the end of the table with folded hands, nodding.

"Shall we say thank you to mother for a lovely meal," he says and gets up.

There comes a scraping of chairs and words in praise of the meal throughout the room. In the sitting room, Agnes is already sitting at the piano: they are going to dance.

"I don't know whether you have seen Ida," says Louise to her mother. "She makes me want to sink into the ground."

Ida leads with the lieutenant.

"Put some life into it," shouts Miss Agnes from the piano. She plays a polka with such energy that the strings vibrate.

Bai dances with Katinka until they have to do a round of the rooms; holding each other by the hand, they dance out through the doors.

Old Linde leads the dance with a gasping Jensen.

"Linde, Linde," shouts Mrs Linde, "Remember your old legs."

Miss Agnes bangs the keys enough to make the rafters ring.

"Good Lord, this will be the death of me," says Helene from the mill.

Suddenly, the chain breaks and the couples, out of breath, sit down on the chairs round about.

"Wow, that warmed us up," says Bai to the lieutenant, wiping his brow.

"Let's see if we can find a beer."

The lieutenant agrees. They go out through the rooms. The beers are all arranged by one of the windows.

"Is it a local beer?" says the lieutenant.

"No, it's a Carlsberg."

"That's good enough for me."

"There's a nice cosy corner here," said Bai. They went into the minister's study, a small room with the collected works of Oehlenschläger and Mynster on green-painted bookshelves and Thorvaldsen's *Christ* on the writing desk.

They settled down at the table with the beer.

"Aye, I could see it all," said Bai. "I could see what was going on. But I thought, let him have his fun, that's what I thought, and her, too."

"Aye, hell of a girl. She's got damned fine breasts. And she does go it when she dances, stationmaster. Leans on one rather nicely."

"Aye, what the hell's she to do, poor girl," said Bai, emptying his beer.

"But what sort of a girl is she?" said the lieutenant. He meant Miss Agnes.

"Nice girl," said Bai.

"No, nothing to be had there," he added. "Friend of my wife."

"Oh, I see," said the lieutenant. "Yes, I thought as much: talks a lot. One of those."

The conversation moved onto more general topics: "These village girls, generally speaking," the lieutenant thought, "they're alright. But you see, stationmaster, they've no culture. Now, town girls, you know, they are something quite different."

The lieutenant had "got hold of something".

"You see, we live in the right district. That's where they have put the castle. You have to live there, either in Frederiksberg or Vesterbro."

"But what kind of girls are they?" said Bai.

"Nice little lasses, by Gad, nice little lasses."

"Well, I don't know. I'm a married man, you know, lieutenant. Goods just to look at, you know, goods just to look at even if one were over there for a couple of days."

"Goods just to look at," he repeated once more.

"Believe me, nice little lasses," said the lieutenant. "Educated girls."

"But they are all said to go off to Russia."

"Yes, so they say."

Mr Linde came in now. "Oh, this is where you are sitting, stationmaster," he said as he walked through the room.

"Yes, vicar, we are sitting here philosophising a little, just quietly over a beer we have stolen."

"Help yourselves; it's nice in here." The minister turned around in the doorway: "They are playing forfeits in there," he said.

Bai and the lieutenant joined the game of forfeits.

They were playing a kissing game.

The little student won and *fell* for Katinka.

"The forfeit's a kiss," shouted Miss Agnes.

Katinka turned her cheek so that the "fruit" could be kissed. His cheeks went very red and he virtually kissed her on her nose.

Katinka laughed and clapped her hands: "I'm falling, I'm falling."

"For Huus," she said.

Huus came and bent. He kissed her hair.

"I'm falling for Miss Jensen," he said. His voice broke as

though he was hoarse.

Miss Jensen was still thinking about that kiss when she was back at home in bed with Bel-Ami.

Katinka supported herself by letting her thoughts rest a little on the radical student.

The guests had left.

Miss Agnes stood in the hall surveying the battleground. Not a single thing was where it should be. There were glasses standing in the corners on the floor. And pudding plates had been put out of the way on the bookcase.

"Ugh," she said, "it looks a bit like the entrance to a certain place down below."

Mr Andersen, the curate, had entered. "Well," she said, "You have been rather nice this evening."

"Miss Agnes, do you find it amusing?"

"No."

"Then why do you do it?"

"I'll tell you why I do it. It's because it amuses the others. But you always want to have fun on your own."

"Give me a hand now," she said, "so we can tidy things up a bit." And she started moving the furniture back into place.

"Mother, I'm never going out with Ida again," said Louise. "I just won't, and I'm telling you that now. It's a scandal, the way she behaves in front of others."

"Just because you're a wallflower, I suppose you think I should keep you company, don't you?"

The widow never interfered in their quarrels. She knew there was nothing she could do about it as she put her curlers in her hair. Then she went around quietly, folding their clothes.

"Carrying on like that makes you damned tired," said Bai. His legs were quite stiff as they walked along together.

Katinka made no reply. They walked along the road home in silence.

III

Spring had arrived.

One afternoon, the parson's daughter fetched Katinka and they went for a walk along the river. Wee Bentzen had knocked up a bench under a couple of willows close to the railway bridge. They sat there and worked until the afternoon train came. The guards on this stretch knew them and waved to them.

"The best thing would be to leave," said Agnes Linde, watching the train as it moved away. "I think about it every day."

"Oh, but, Agnes…"

"Yes, that would be the best thing – for both of us – that either he or I should go away."

And they discuss this eternal subject for the thousandth time.

It was a day in the middle of winter. Agnes Linde and the curate went past on their way from the pond, where they had been skating, and the curate had to go into the station to send a letter and he fell into conversation with Bai.

Agnes came into the living room with her skates over her arm. She was very brusque and simply replied "Yes" and "No" to whatever Katinka said. Then, after standing over by the window and looking out, she suddenly burst into tears.

"What is it, Miss Linde? Are you ill?" said Katinka going over to her and putting an arm round her. "What on earth is wrong?"

Agnes Linde battled with her tears. But her weeping only increased. She moved Katinka's arm.

"Let me go in here," she said, moving over towards the bedroom.

There she threw herself on the bed and told Katinka all about it in a torrent of words, how she loved Andersen, but he only played about with her, and she could take no more.

Since that day, Katinka had enjoyed the confidence of the parson's daughter.

Katinka was used to being taken into people's confidence. It had been like that when she was a young girl at home, too. Bleeding hearts would all come to her. It was presumably because of her quiet manner and because she herself never said much. She was the ideal person for listening to others.

The parson's daughter came almost every day and she spent hours with Katinka. It was the same thing time after time: her love and him. And every day she told things as though they were new, even though she had already told them a thousand times over.

Then, when she had sat talking for three or four hours and had finally started to weep, Agnes packed her sewing up:

"Yes, we are indeed an odd couple," she said in conclusion.

Now that spring had come, they sat down by the stream.

Agnes talked and Katinka listened. She sat with her hands on her lap, looking out across the meadows. There was a slight haze out there, and the hollow looked like a big, blue lake. There was no seeing what was lake and what was sky; it was all just like one dawning blue. With the groups of willows like islands in the sea.

Agnes told about the early days when she had come home from Copenhagen and met Andersen. Months had passed, and she had simply not realised she was fond of him.

Katinka listened and did not listen. She knew the theme and she nodded silently.

But bit by bit she had learned of the other's love. She knew it and all the emotions that accompanied it. She shared them as though they were her own. Of course, they never talked about anything else.

And she felt comfortable with all these words of love. Her thoughts became so familiar with everything that belonged to love, at least in these two strangers.

After accompanying Agnes Linde part of the way and then returning home herself, she could sit for half an hour at a time in the summer house by the elder tree out in the garden. And it was as though all those words of love floated in the air about her, and she heard them again and reflected on them.

It was in keeping with her quiet, rather passive nature that words and thoughts with which she was now so familiar as it were should return time and time again, on the road, on her way home.

And they cocooned her. They turned into dreams that led her far away, into realms of which she was scarcely aware.

Life had also been quieter at home recently. Huus was not coming so frequently now spring had arrived. He said there was so much to do.

When he came, his mood varied so much as well. It was often as though he simply failed to notice how pleased Katinka was to see him, and he chatted mostly with Bai although Katinka had had so much to tell him and to ask him about.

Just now in spring, when there had been so much to arrange

and change everywhere.

But there was something wrong. Perhaps he was not happy working for Kiær on the farm; it was said that he was a little difficult to get on with.

And indeed, she herself was also occasionally rather low spirited.

But perhaps that was the result of not getting enough sleep.

She stayed in the living room in the evening when Bai went to undress. He would then wander around half naked for a long time and then sit on the edge of the bed and talk and talk.

Katinka found it wearisome that he would never settle down and stop chattering.

And when she herself finally got to bed and lay there in the darkness beside the soundly sleeping Bai, she was unable to fall asleep and had a sense of malaise that prompted her to get up again and go into the living room. And there she sat, by the window. The night train rushed past and a great silence once more lay over the fields. No sound, not the slightest breeze in the summer night. The first grey light of day came; and a cold, damp air rose from the meadows.

And it grew lighter and lighter as the larks began to sing.

Huus had told her how fond he was of watching the arrival of morning.

He had told her what it was like in the mountains when morning came. It was like a mighty sea of gold and red, he said, with the mountain tops standing there half gold and half pink. And the peaks floated there like islands in a vast ocean.

And then, bit by bit, he said, it was as though all the mountain tops came on fire.

And then the sun came.

And rose.

And swept the darkness out of the valleys as though with

the wave of a great wing.

He would often talk about that sort of thing now, about all those memories from his travels.

In general, he talked more now, that is if he talked at all.

It grew quite light, and Katinka still sat by the window. But she must presumably get some sleep.

The air was heavy in the bedroom, and Bai lay there and had thrown the blankets off.

When Huus came of an evening, they would mostly sit in the summer house by the elder tree.

They watched the eight o'clock train leave. The odd farmer would saunter out onto the platform and greet them as he passed them and drove home.

Then they went down into the garden. The cherry trees were in blossom. The white petals drifted like some brightly glistening rain through the summer air down on to the lawn.

They sat still, looking out at the white trees. It was as though the gentle evening silence that had descended upon the wold was enveloping everything. Up in the village a gate could be heard closing. Cattle were lowing over the fields.

Katinka talked of her home.

About her friends and her brothers and the old house's courtyard, where there were so many pigeons.

"And then, in the new flat with mother... after father's death."

"Yes, that was a happy time."

"But then I got married of course."

Huus looked out across the soft snow of fruit blossom gently falling on the grass.

"There was Thora Berg, she was great fun. In the evening when she was coming home from a party with the entire garrison on her heels, throwing sand at all the windows as she went through the town."

Katinka sat for a while.

"She is married now as well," she said.

"And they say she has several children."

A man passed by on the road outside. "Good evening," he said over the hedge.

"Good evening, Kristen Peter."

"Good evening," said Katinka.

"Hmm," said Katinka again, "the last time I saw her was at my wedding. All the girls sang at it; they were all up near the organ, in the choir loft. I can still see them, all their faces, all of them. But I wept so much."

Huus still said nothing and she could not see his face. He was bending forward as he sat there, studying something down on the ground.

"That was almost eleven years ago," said Katinka. "Yes. Time passes."

"Yes, when you are happy," said Huus without stirring.

Katinka did not hear this at first. Then it was as though the words suddenly struck her.

"Yes," she said, starting a little.

And then, before long: "This is my home now."

Again, they sat in silence.

Bai came out into the garden. He could be heard from far away. He always made such a noise, and before this it had been so quiet in the dusk.

"I'll fetch the glasses," said Katinka.

"Aye, a lovely evening," said Bai. "Lovely evening out in the open."

Katinka returned with glasses and a bottle.

"I've had a visitor," said Bai.

"Who?"

"Miss Ida. She's off again now."

"What, Ida?"

"Aye," Bai laughed: "They've given up on Miss Louise by god, and now they are raising all the sails on the lighter vessel. She's going to stay away all summer."

"Aye, well, it'd be nice if one of them was successful." Bai sat for a while: "Aye, but what the hell. A girl like that has to get married."

Bai often lectured on marriage. He was something of a philosopher when it came to that subject.

"I joined the railways," he said. "Do you think it was because I wanted to? There was simply no future as a lieutenant. That's what it's like, there's no getting away from it: girls just have to be taken to the altar. Then it works out. We all see that, you know. They get used to living together. They have a house and home, and then the children arrive."

"For most people," Bai concluded with something approaching a sigh.

They sat in silence; it had grown quite dark beneath the elder tree.

The end of June arrived.

"Our lovely lady looks a bit pale about the gills," said Agnes Linde when she came down to the station.

"Yes, I don't think the heat suits me," said Katinka. It was as though there was something restive about her and she was constantly starting on something and then abandoning it again and then coming and going.

She liked best to be sitting with Agnes down by the stream. She looked out across the fields and always heard the same things.

Agnes Linde always adopted a quite different, gentle voice when she spoke about him, "her man", as she called him.

Katinka sat looking at her as she sat there with her head bowed and she smiled.

"And then one snivels," said Agnes. "Monstrous as it is, this is perhaps the best I can expect."

"Yes," said Katinka, still looking at her.

When Agnes Linde did not come to her, Katinka went up to the parsonage. She really longed to hear her speak.

And then she saw Andersen as well. She saw them together, Agnes and him.

She stood there while they played croquet on the big lawn. She stood and watched them, these two, who loved each other.

She listened to them inquisitively and watched them almost as though they were some great wonder.

And one day, she wept as she went home.

Huus' visits were so irregular now. Sometimes he would come twice in the course of one day and would hardly sit down in the garden house before he had to get up on his horse again. And sometimes several days would elapse during which they hardly saw him at the station.

The hay had been cut and was now in stacks all over the meadows. There was a constant fragrance in the air.

One evening, Huus was in a good mood and suggested they should have a "day at the big fair". They could drive there in a carriage and first have a brief rest in the woods and then see all the splendours of the fair.

Bai thought it a good idea, and the outing was planned. They were to start out early in the morning while it was still cool and they would not come home until that night or the following morning.

Just the Bais and Huus.

Katinka was busy all day making preparations.

She studied her cookery book and made plans during the night and went to town to do her shopping.

Just as the train was leaving, Huus came to fetch the post.

"Huus," she shouted from the carriage window.

"Where are you going?" he shouted.

"Shopping. Marie is with me." And she pulled Marie across and showed her face at the window. "Goodbye."

"Hmm," said Bai. "Katinka's gone quite crazy. She's frying and boiling things for that trip as though she was getting us ready to withstand a cholera epidemic."

In town they had started erecting tents in the streets and up on the market place the horses for the merry-go-rounds were lined up in rows against the churchyard wall. Katinka went in among the fairground people, who were hammering and banging, and looked at all that was going on. She stared at the crates and gazed in wonder at each piece of canvas that was raised up.

"Would you mind, miss."

She had to jump across both boards and ropes.

"They are calling me miss," she said.

"I just hope the weather holds, Marie," she said.

They went out along the streets to the park. There was a caravan there. The men were asleep by the roadside; the wife of one of them was washing stockings in a bowl on the lowered steps. Three pairs of unmentionables were stretched out and flapping on a line.

Katinka looked inquisitively at the woman and the men at the roadside.

"Do you want something?" shouted the woman in some foreign accent.

"Ugh," shouted Katrina. She was quite afraid and ran a little further away.

"That was the Strong Woman," she said.

They wandered further along the road. At the edge of the park a group of joiners were laying the dance floor. It was cool in there beneath the trees after the sun-drenched road. Katinka sat down on a bench.

"This is where we are going to dance," she said.

"Yes, Huus must be a good dancer," said Marie. She was a constant and loyal admirer of Huus; a photograph of him framed in velvet stood on her chest of drawers and she had an old visiting card with his name as a bookmark in her hymn book. Peter the porter attended to her more tangible needs.

Katinka made no reply. She just sat there watching the people at work.

"Let's hope the weather holds," she said to one of them.

"Yes," he said, looking up into the trees. He could not see the sky as he wiped his brow with his sleeve, "it all depends on that."

Katinka and Marie went back. It was high time. They crossed the square. The evening bells in the church tower could be heard ringing above the din in the market.

They spent the final day baking. Katinka wore a short-sleeved dress and kneaded so that her hair was covered with flour like that of a miller.

"No one's allowed in. No one's allowed in." Someone was knocking on the door, which was locked.

Katinka thought it was Huus.

"It's me," shouted Agnes Linde. "What is going on?"

She came in and helped with the baking. It was a pound cake that needed to be stirred and stirred for ever. "It's for

Huus," said Katinka. "He's got a sweet tooth so I'm making a pound cake for him."

Agnes stirred until the dough bobbled. "Aye, menfolk must have their pound cake," she said.

Katinka took the tray out. "Have a taste," she said. "Be careful not to burn your tongue." Her face was as red as a copper pan straight out of the oven.

Miss Jensen and Louise came down for the afternoon train. They knocked on the kitchen window and stood talking outside.

"Good Lord, they must have smelt it," said Agnes Linde. She dropped her tired arms and sat with the mixing bowl between legs that were spread rather inelegantly.

Marie took a plate out onto the platform so they could have a taste.

Louise was overwhelmed with such joy while sitting on the platform bench, that a couple of commission agents in the train saw a significant bit of her beauty.

When the train had left, those working in the kitchen opened the windows. Louise and little Miss Jensen munched away happily on the bench outside.

"You have been so fortunate, Mrs Bai – wonderful."

"Yes, Mrs Bai is an excellent housewife," said Miss Jensen.

"Now we are off again," said Agnes inside the kitchen. She set about the dough.

Bai opened the office window above the platform bench.

"There you are," he said. "And here am I without anything at all."

"Would you like a bit, Mr Bai?" asked Louise. "Do you like sweet things as well?"

"If anyone deigned to offer me some," said Bai, adopting his club tone.

There was a din on the platform, accompanied by squeaks. "What is going on?" asked Agnes from the kitchen.

"We're feeding the birds," shouted Louise. She had jumped up on the bench in all her beauty and stood there putting cake into Bai's mouth.

"Oh, he's biting," she screams.

It was on such occasions that Mrs Abel would say, "They just go on playing like children, without knowing anything of the world."

Louise took the empty plate back. She picked up the crumbs with her finger tips. Louise and Ida were always like that: they never wasted anything.

She stood at the kitchen window and looked inside.

"Mother should have known about this," she said in a sweet voice.

"Oh, so she hasn't got wind of it," said Agnes over the pound cake.

Louise was given a bag of cakes through the window. "It's something to take home," she said as she came out on to the road with little Miss Jensen.

She and Miss Jensen had eaten the cakes before they were past the wood. Louise threw the paper away.

"Good heavens, my dear Louise, Miss Linde might see you with those sharp eyes of hers."

Miss Jensen picked the paper up. Down in her pocket, she quietly wrapped it round three cakes for Bel-Ami.

Katinka started to feel tired. She sat on the chopping block with her sleeves rolled up and surveyed her work.

"But it's nothing to what we used to do at home, nothing compared to when we did our Christmas baking."

She told how they used to bake, her mother and her sisters and the entire household. How she used to make dough into pig shapes and then how they popped when they were dropped in the hot fat.

And her brothers, how they used to pinch bits so that mother had to wield a wooden spoon to guard the stone jar containing cake mixture.

And if they were paring almonds they stole so many there would not even be fifty left out of a pound.

There was a knock on the door. It was Huus.

"No one is coming in," said Katinka at the door. "In an hour. Come back in an hour."

Huus appeared outside the window. "You can wait in the garden," said Katinka. She hurried to finish and sent Agnes down to keep Huus company.

Agnes stayed there for about an hour. Then she left.

"Mr Huus is too easy to keep company," she said to Andersen. "All he wants is for you to stay quiet so he can whistle in peace."

"Where is Agnes?" said Katinka when she went down into the garden.

"I think she left."

"But when?"

"I suppose it was about an hour ago."

Huus laughed. "Miss Linde and I are so fond of each other," he said. "But we don't exactly have much to say to each other."

"We must pack the things," said Katinka.

They went indoors and started packing the big basket. They stuffed hay into it to be sure the jars were firmly fixed in place.

"Tighter," said Katinka, "tighter." And she pressed firmly on Huus' hands.

She opened the bureau and counted the right number of spoons and forks from the cutlery drawer.

"And I'm going to take a fan," she said.

She started to search. "Oh, it's in this drawer."

It was in the drawer with all the petticoats and the bridal veil. She opened the box containing the old bits of ribbon. "Look," she said. "All that old rubbish."

She plunged her hand down into the box and rummaged around in all kinds of ribbons and decorations. All that old rubbish.

Again she looked for her fan.

"Oh, will you just hold my veil?" she said. She put her bridal veil and a fine shawl over Huus' arm. "There it is," she said. The fan was at the bottom of the drawer.

"And your shawl," she said. It was on one side, packed in tissue paper. She took it out.

Huus had been holding so tight on the yellowing bridal veil that he left marks on the lace.

The evening train arrived, and they went out onto the platform.

"Phew," said the slim guard in the tight, revealing trousers, "getting the train through during the holidays... half an hour late..."

"You're in for trouble," said Bai.

Katinka looked down at the carriages. There was a sweaty face at each window.

"Fancy," she said, "all these people wanting to travel." The guard gave a laugh.

"Well," he said. "That's what the railways are for." He saluted and jumped on to the footboard.

The train left. The young guard continued to lean out and nod.

Katinka waved her blue shawl. Suddenly, all the people going on holiday waved and nodded back at her from the carriage windows, all laughing and enjoying themselves.

Katinka shouted and waved her blue shawl, and they waved

back from the train as long as they could be seen.

Huus went home after tea. He was to come to the station at six o'clock the following morning.

Katinka stood in the garden behind the hedge and sang out:

"Cricket, oh cricket, now bring us good weather."

The scent of the trees in the grove descended on her. She stood there, smiling and staring up into the blue air.

"Curious how blue suits the little lady," thought the railway guard with the tight, revealing trousers. He was always on the lookout for anything interesting along this stretch of the track.

"We must get up at five o'clock," said Bai in the direction of the kitchen.

"Yes, all right, Bai, I'm coming." Katinka scraped a bit of black away from the pound cake. "We have to get everything ready, you know."

She wrapped the pound cake up and examined the basket one last time. She opened the door to the courtyard and stood there looking out. The only sound was that of the pigeons cooing up there.

The last pale traces of red were disappearing in the west. The stream wound its way and disappeared among the steaming meadows.

How she loved that spot.

She closed the door and went inside.

Bai had put his watch down near the lighted lamp by the bed. He wanted to check when she had finished fiddling about.

But he had fallen asleep and lay there sweating and breathing heavily through his nose in the light from the lamp.

Katinka quietly put it out. She undressed in the dark.

Katinka was in the garden when the carriage arrived. Her blue dress could be recognised all the way from the turning.

"Good morning, good morning, you are bringing a fine day with you."

She ran out onto the platform. "He's here," she shouted.

"The hampers, Marie."

Bai stood in his shirt sleeves at the bedroom window. "Morning, Huus. Looks as though we're going to get sunstroke, doesn't it."

"Oh, there's a bit of a breeze, you know" said Huus, alighting from the carriage.

They managed to secure the baskets and had coffee out on the platform. Wee Bentzen was so sleepy that Bai made him run up and down the platform three times to wake him up.

Katinka promised to bring some cake back for him, and they climbed into the carriage. Bai wanted to be in charge of the horses and sat on the front seat together with Marie, whose dress was so starched that it crackled at the slightest movement.

Katinka looked like a young girl in her big white sunhat.

"They will be sending food from the inn for you," Katinka said to Wee Bentzen .

"Well we'd better be off now, then," said Bai. Wee Bentzen ran into the garden and waved eagerly.

They drove some way along a narrow road through the meadows. It was still quite cool, with a good-natured summer breeze; the clover and the damp grass filled the air with perfume.

"It is so lovely and fresh," said Katinka.

"Yes, a wonderful morning," said Huus.

"Lovely fresh air." Bai gently tapped the horses.

They drove along the avenue past Kiær's land. The cattleman's hut was out there on its wheels surrounded by the cattle. A dog barked from far away as it rounded up some cattle; the great cows raised their thick necks and lowed, lazy and replete.

Katinka looked out across the green meadow with its scattered, shiny cattle, all illumined by the sun.

"It's so lovely," she said.

"Yes, isn't it," said Huus turning his head towards her. "It's beautiful."

They started to talk. They saw the same things and took pleasure in the same things. The same things always caught their attention. And then either he or Katinka would nod.

Bai talked to the horses like an old cavalryman.

No more than an hour had passed before he started to talk of "having a bite".

"Early mornings make their demands on you, Tik," he said. "You need something to keep you going, damn it."

Katinka really could not unpack now. And where were they going to find a place to sit in any case?

But Bai did not give up, and they came to a standstill by a field where the rye had been stacked.

They took one of the hampers from the carriage and sat down on a stack close to the roadside.

Bai ate as though he had not seen food for a week.

"Cheers, Huus," he said. "Good company."

They chatted and passed the jars around and ate.

"This does you good, you know, Tik," said Bai.

People passed by and glanced at them.

"Enjoy your breakfast," they said and walked on.

"Cheers, Huus. Here's to a good day."

"Thank you, Mrs Bai."

"That bucked us up," said Bai. They were in the carriage again. "But it's going to be a hot one today, isn't it Marie?"

"Yes," said Marie, glistening with perspiration. "It's

pretty warm."

"We'll soon be getting to the woods," said Huus.

They drove on. The edge of the woods was over there, bluish in the heat.

"Don't the fir trees smell wonderful?" said Katinka.

They reached the edge of the woods, and densely packed fir trees threw shadows over much of the road ahead. They all breathed a sigh of relief, but they did not speak as they drove slowly through the forest. The fir trees stood in long, straight rows away from the road and disappeared into the gloom of the forest. And there were no birds, no singing, no noise.

Only great clouds of insects could be seen rising from the fir trees up into the light.

They emerged from the woods again.

"Pretty solemn in there, isn't it," said Bai, breaking the silence.

They reached the beech forest towards midday and went into the forester's house.

Bai said, "It's good to get a bit of exercise. One has to stretch one's legs, Huus." And he immediately went and sat down beneath a tree to have a snooze.

Huus helped with the unpacking. "You have such good fingers, Huus," said Katinka. Marie went backwards and forwards, warming the pots in hot water in the kitchen.

"My mother-in-law always said that," said Huus.

"Mother-in-law?"

"Yes," said Huus. "My fiancée's mother."

Katinka said nothing. Knives and forks rattled out of the paper she was holding.

"Yes," said Huus, "I've never talked about it. I was engaged once."

"Oh? I didn't know."

Katinka arranged the knives. Marie returned.

"We could go down to the pond," said Huus.

"Yes, if Marie will call us." They went down the path into the woods. The pond was a small marsh lake a little way into the wood. The trees stretched their great tops out over the dark water.

They had not spoken on the way there. Now they sat beside each other on a bench by the lake.

"No," said Huus. "I've never talked about it."

Katinka looked out across the water in silence.

"It was my mother," he said, "who so much wanted it. For the sake of the future."

"Oh," said Katinka.

"And so it went on for a whole year until she broke it off."

Huus spoke jerkily, with long pauses, as though ashamed or angry.

"That's what engagements and marriages are like," he said again.

A bird started warbling over there in the forest. Katinka heard every note in the silence.

"And I suppose I was a coward as well and went on with it," said Huus again. "Stuck there really and truly like a coward. Day after day. I stayed with it," he spoke quietly, "until she broke it off. Because she was fond of me."

Katinka placed her hand in a gentle caress down on his, which he was pressing hard on the bench.

"Poor Huus," was all she said.

And she sat patting his hand, gently and soothingly: that poor man, how he had suffered.

They sat like that, close to each other. The midday heat descended on the waters of the tiny lake. Clouds of midges and flies filled the air with their buzzing.

They spoke no more. Marie's shouting roused them.

"They are calling us," said Katinka.

They rose and silently went along the path.

They were all rather merry at table. Finally they had some old Aalborg port wine with the pound cake.

Bai sat in his shirt sleeves, every other minute saying, "Aye, children, our green Danish forest is a damned nice place to be in."

He was overcome by an attack of tenderness and wanted Katinka to sit on his knee. She tore herself away. "What are you thinking of, Bai," she said. She had turned pale and blushed at the same time.

"I suppose she's shy in front of strangers," said Bai.

All had gone quiet. Katinka started to pack the baskets and Huus rose.

"Aye," said Bai. "What about a bit of a walk to let the lunch go down?" He put on his coat. "It's good for the digestion, you know."

"Yes," said Katinka. "You could go for a walk while I pack up."

Huus and Bai strolled down the road, Bai walking with his hat in his hand, feeling warm from the heat and the old port.

"There you are, Huus; that's marriage for you, my lad," he said. "That's what it's like and it's never any different."

"It's no damned good. Everything they write about and everything you sit and mop up in your weeklies about marriage and chastity and all that. And faithfulness and the 'needs' they pontificate about, just like old Linde and his Lord's Prayer. They put it all fine and it sounds so good, and it gives people something to write about. But you see it doesn't really get down to things, Huus."

He stopped and waved his straw hat in front of Huus.

"Well, you saw now. I have needs but Katinka won't... A lovely summer's day when you've had a good meal out in the country and yet even so, she wouldn't even give me a kiss. That's what women are like. You can never reckon with them. They're like that at times, you see, Huus."

"Between ourselves," Bai shook his head. "It's damned difficult for a man in the prime of life."

Huus hit out at some nettles with his walking stick. He swung it with such force that they went down as though they had been mown.

"Aye, that's what it's like," said Bai, walking along and looking dubious, "but they don't say anything about that in the weeklies. But as one grown man to another, we know where the shoe pinches."

They heard Katinka call out behind them, and Huus replied with a shout that echoed right through the forest.

Katinka had recovered her spirits. It would be a good idea for them to have a nap under the trees now, she said. She knew of a spot, a lovely spot beneath an oak tree. And she went ahead of them to find it.

Huus followed. He made a sound like a cuckoo in the direction of the trees. Bai heard him laughing and yodelling.

"Aye," he said, "he can laugh all right. He's free of all this."

It was not long before Bai was asleep beneath the great oak tree with his nose in the air and his hat lying on his stomach.

"You must have a sleep now, Huus," said Katinka.

"Ye-es" said Huus. They were sitting each on their own side of the oak trunk.

Katinka had taken her straw hat off and leant her head against the tree. She sat looking up into the oak. Right up there at the top, the sunbeams were like drops of shining gold in the greenery, and the birds were singing in the undergrowth.

"It's so lovely here," she whispered, bending her head forward.

"Yes, it's lovely," whispered Huus. He sat with his arms round his knees, staring up into the treetop.

It was so quiet. They could both hear Bai's breathing; they watched an insect buzzing its way up into the green treetop and the birds that were chirping both so close to them and yet so far away.

"Are you asleep?" Katinka whispered.

"Yes," said Huus.

They sat again for a while. Huus listened, rose quietly and moved forward. Yes, she was asleep. She looked like a child, with her head on one side and her mouth slightly open as though smiling in her sleep.

Huus stood looking at her for a long time. Then he quietly returned to his place, and happily, with his eyes trained on the top of the oak tree, he listened to her sleeping.

When Marie woke them with some robust shouts of "hello", summoning them to coffee, Bai had slept off his irritation along with the old port wine.

"A cognac does you good out in the open," he said. "A nice little cognac in the open air."

Bai was again able to manage a piece of pound cake with the cognac. Bai was a man able to consume vast quantities.

"Lovely cake," he said.

"It's Huus' cake," said Katinka.

"Oh well," said Bai. "Provided the rest of us are allowed to eat it."

After coffee, they drove on. Bai was tired of holding the reins and he took Huus' place on the back seat with Katinka. They were all a little lethargic. The hot summer sun was blazing down on them and the road was dusty. Katinka sat looking at the back of Huus' head, his broad neck well browned by the sun.

The hotel courtyard was tightly packed with carriages that had been left there. Women and girls who had just descended from the wagon seats were shaking their skirts and smoothing them down. All the windows in the basement were open; a plentiful supply of hot punch was being passed among the card players. A falsetto with piano was busy playing a popular song in the main wing behind rolled blinds.

"That's one of Agnes's songs," said Katinka.

"It's the Nightingales," said Bai. "We'll have to go in and hear them chirp this evening."

Katinka kept close to the main wing as they walked. But there was nothing to be seen.

"No peeping," said Bai. "Pay at the entrance."

Inside, behind the curtains, a screechy woman's voice started imploring "O Charles, my dear".

"Oh Charles, my dear,
Please write to me…"

"Oh," said Katinka, standing by the window and nodding. "That's the one Agnes sings."

"That's where you always wrote…"

"Come on, Tik," said Bai. "Just you go with Huus. I'll barge a way through if there's a crowd."

"But the first verse is the only one we know by heart," said Katinka, listening as she took Huus' arm.

"That's where you always wrote…"

implored the screeching voice.

"The other songs all say more or less the same," said Huus.

"Are you coming?" shouted Bai.

Outside the entrance a gangling woman was singing about the mass murderer Thomas, beating his likeness with a cane. The audience stood there sheepishly, repeating the refrain lingeringly just like singing the amen in church.

Long rows of wooden-faced girls walked arm in arm, waiting to be picked out by the boys standing in groups in front of the tents, smoking pipes and with hands buried deep in trouser pockets.

One lad stepped forward.

"Hello, Mary," he said. And Mary reached him the tip of her fingers. "Hello, Søren," she said. And the entire line of girls stopped and waited.

Søren stood in front of Mary for a moment, looking first at his pipe and then at his boots. "Goodbye, Mary," he said.

"Goodbye, Søren."

And Søren rejoined his group, and the row of girls closed again, and they continued with their mouths primly closed.

"Damn stupid way of carrying on," said Bai, "blocking the street."

The married women gathered in groups, standing there looking each other up and down with melancholy mien as though waiting for a corpse. When they spoke, they whispered so it was difficult to hear them, as though they could not really open their mouths properly, and when they had said a couple of words, they stood there again in silence and looked quietly offended.

It was impossible to make any progress. "I'll use my

elbows," said Katinka. She was constantly being pushed in against Huus.

"Just keep close to me," said Huus.

It was impossible to hear anything with the gangling female singing about the mass murderer and a couple of barrel organs that forlornly mingled General Bertrand's song of departure with the Ajaxes' duet. The grammar school pupils weaved their ways in and out, whistling through their fingers, and lethargic village kids blew up balloons and made them screech while gazing in the air with immovable expressions on their faces.

The sun shone straight down on the street, baking both people and honey cakes.

"Ugh, it's hot," said Katinka.

"This is where we can get waffles," shouted Bai.

"Waffles, ladies, waffles, made by Tyrolese Ferdinand's brown-eyed daughter."

"Waffles, Huus, waffles," said Katinka, forcing her way through a wall of girls who were blocking the street.

The girls squealed. Ooh, the boys from the grammar school had sewn their skirts together.

"It's all those grammar school lads," shouted a couple of louts from the council school. They were pinning them with safety pins.

The girls gathered in a group to undo themselves. "Ooh," they howled. "Ooh." The boys from the grammar school saw their chance and broke in like lightning to pinch their legs.

"Ooh." They howled at the top of their voices. Katinka shouted along with them out of sheer giddiness.

"Waffles, ladies, made by Tyrolese Ferdinand's brown-eyed daughter."

They went over to the oven: "Three waffles, sir, Dutch ones, fifteen øre."

"Will you sprinkle some sugar on it, brown-eyes."

The brown-eyed one sprinkled some sugar with her bare fingers:

"Aye, madam," said the man, "she has known better days."

"What about a tip," he bleated across the street, "for Tyrolese Ferdinand's brown-eyed daughter?"

The brown-eyed daughter automatically rattled a collection box she was holding out and looked as though she neither heard nor saw.

"Sugar, brown-eyes."

Again the brown-eyed daughter's fingers dipped into the sugar.

They reached the market place. "It's almost enough to deafen you," said Katinka, putting her hands to her ears. Le Tort, the great professor of conjuring, stood on some high scaffolding, struggling with two trombones and competing with the music emitted by three merry-go-rounds. A white-painted Pierrot dragged a big bass drum up in front of the biggest arena in the world:

"The biggest arena, ladies and gentlemen, the world-famous arena."

He made music by putting the hindmost part of his body down hard on his drum.

"Miss Flora, Miss Flora, the high trapeze."

It was just in front of them. "Miss Flora, the Queen of the Air, gentlemen, ten øre." The barker swung a great bell with his right arm.

"The Queen of the Air, ten øre."

Professor Le Tort was determined. He proclaimed all sorts of wonders, his voice cracking, and he decided to make five hundred yards of silk ribbon for free. He started regurgitating up there on his scaffolding and pulling strips of tissue paper out of his throat, all the while turning so red faced that he looked as though he was about to have a fit.

"The Queen of the Air, ten øre."

In the biggest arena in the world, Pierrot was standing on his head on a drum and beating it with the top of his head.

The merry-go-rounds were going to the accompaniment of brass bands and barrel organs.

"Ladies, the Queen of the Air. The Queen of the Air, ten øre."

The sun baked down on them, the air was filled with the scent of honey cake and there were milling crowds and a great din.

"Isn't it lovely," said Katinka. She looked up at Huus and shook herself a little, like a kitten in scorching heat.

"That's his wife," she said.

"Who?" asked Huus.

"The one that was doing the washing."

It was the Queen of the Air going up the steps with pink legs in laced boots and a broad, waggling backside.

"Miss Flora, known as the Queen of the Air, ten øre."

The Queen of the Air was equipped with a fan which she handled like a fig leaf; she munched a few plums in preparation for going inside and up in the air.

"Shall we go in?" said Katinka.

"Tik," shouted Bai. He wanted to see the Snake Lady. They pushed their way forward through the crush and passed a merry-go-round. Marie was riding a lion, half on the lap of a cavalryman.

Katinka also wanted to have a ride. Bai said that on no account was he going to pay money to be made sick. Katinka found a horse on the inside alongside Huus. They started to move, slowly and then faster. She nodded to Bai and laughed at all the faces revolving around them.

"What a crowd," she said. She could see over all their heads.

They had a second ride. "Hold tight," said Katinka, leaning forward across Huus.

"Be careful," he said, putting his arm round her.

Katinka smiled and leaned back. All the faces started to merge into one for her. They were simply a mass of black and white that kept on whirling around.

She continued to smile as she closed her eyes.

It was as though all the noise from the fair and the music and the voices and the blaring horns combined in one intense sound in her ears, while everything rocked gently.

She opened her eyes a little: "I can't see anything," she said and closed them again.

The bell rang and they started to move more slowly. "Let's have another turn," she said. Huus had leant in towards her. She did not realise that she was supporting herself on his shoulder. "Catch it," she said. They flew past the ring, and she laughed in his face.

She sat with half open eyes looking into the circle of people. It was as though all the faces had been threaded on a string.

Though dizzy, she caught sight of Marie. She had come up again and was sitting in a carriage with her cavalryman.

She was sitting on his knee.

She looked almost as though she was about to swoon.

And all the others: just see how they were leaning tight against the lads, as though they were half dead.

Katinka suddenly straightened up; all her blood had rushed to her head. The merry-go-round stopped.

"Come on," she said and got down from the horse.

Bai was standing by the ring pole. Katinka took his hand.

"It makes you dizzy," she said, stepping down onto the ground. She was quite pale from having driven around so much.

"You look after Tik, Huus," said Bai. "I'll lead the way." He pinched Marie's arm as she descended from the merry-go-round with her cavalryman.

Marie was embarrassed to see her employer and his family and disentangled herself from her blue-uniformed companion.

"She's getting on fine," said Bai as he set off.

"It's just here," said Katinka. Huus offered her his arm.

The snake lady Miss Theodora was displaying her lethargic pets alongside the merry-go-round. They were fat, slimy creatures that she took out of a box containing blankets. Miss Theodora tickled them under their chins to liven them up a little.

"They are digesting their lunch, miss," said Bai in his club voice.

"What did you say?" said Miss Theodora. "Don't you think they are alive?" Miss Theodora took the reference to digesting their lunch as an insult.

She took the snake by its neck and scratched its head so that it opened its jaws and managed to produce a hiss.

Miss Theodora called it her little pet and held it to her breast. Miss Theodora was of impressive female girth and wore a pageboy suit.

The snake quietly allowed its tail to hang between the lady's knees. "Sweetie," said Miss Theodora.

"Let's go," said Katinka. "It's horrible." She had taken Huus' arm in disgust.

"Yes," said the owner, flattered in her assumption that this was from fear and feeling duly flattered. "Difficult beasts, my dear. But she's tamed lions as well."

Katinka was already outside.

"I don't know how people can do that sort of thing," she said. She was trembling all over.

"Aye," said Bai, passing his hands over it like an expert. The owner had asked the "gentleman" to convince himself that the animals could really move "as well as on a bare body".

"Aye," said Bai. "There's meat on it all right."

The snake lady Theodora gave a conciliated smile as she put her "little dears" back into their box.

"Aye," said its owner, "she used to tame lions, sir."

"For eight years," said Miss Theodora.

Huus and Katinka were on the other side of the square. It was gradually starting to grow dark, and all the barkers were shouting in competition with each other, eagerly and desperately, on the stands.

"Reduced price, reduced price for you, lady," the professor shouted to Katinka. He wiped the sweat off with 'the remarkable handkerchief', "Twenty øre for you and your gentleman friend."

Katinka walked on so much faster that Bai could hardly keep up.

People started to be merrier. Groups of unsteady lads ran singing towards the rows of girls, who screamed and scattered; and couples were gradually starting to flirt in the lanes formed by the tents.

A great noise issued from the refreshment tents and from up where the brown-eyed daughter was pouring cognac on the waffles.

The three policemen hobbled around with their walking sticks. They were men who had been slightly wounded during the wars and who were keeping together to maintain order; here and there, in groups behind the tents, the grammar school boys suddenly started whistling through their fingers and piercing the air above all the din.

It grew darker and darker as Katinka and Huus walked down along the rows of tents, buying this and that.

Storm lanterns were already being lit in the tents, throwing a sparse light over buns and honey cakes. The ladies behind the high counters polished the honey cakes with the flat of their hands making them shine and handed them to Huus and Katinka on a long scoop.

Bai turned up and bought some as well.

Huus had bought Katinka a small Japanese tray as a present from the fair. She gave him a honey cake.

"Hey," said Bai. "Are you giving Huus honey cake? Give him one shaped like a heart."

"Miss," he shouted, "can we have a heart here."

"A heart, sir, with a poem."

"Bai," said Katinka.

"There is going to be a shower," said Huus behind them.

"Blast." Bai turned from the counter.

The first spots fell. "It'll soon be throwing it down," said Bai.

"We can shelter in the panorama," said Huus.

"Yes." Katinka took Bai's arm. "Come on."

Everyone ran to get indoors. Women and girls threw their skirts over their heads and ran off with handkerchiefs arranged in squares over their new hats.

"Look there," said Bai. "My God, petticoats are on show now."

The girls stood around in the doorways, revealing their blue stockings with tops hidden by their Icelandic petticoats.

The tradesfolk dragged their wares under cover, cursing and swearing. The grammar school boys ran all over the place, making a din and getting drenched.

"Here it is," said Katinka.

"All of Italy, ladies and gentlemen, for fifty øre." The man was hoarse and wrapped in woollen scarves: "There we are."

"It's pouring down," said Katinka. She stood at the entrance to the tent and shook herself as she looked out.

The water ran in torrents as though the sluice gates had been opened. Half the market place was already under water. The slightly wounded policemen were running around, limping as they went, under their umbrellas and raising the gutter coverings.

All around, under the tents and in doorways, stood the women, soaked to the skin and looking less than perfect.

Inside the panorama, all was empty and quite quiet. The heavy, monotonous drumming of the rain on the roof could be heard, and then it had become quite cool.

It was as though Katinka caught her breath after all the din.

"Oh, how nice it is here," she said.

"They are country scenes," said Bai, who had started looking in the peepholes.

"Blue water," he said and went on. He preferred to go out into the entrance hall to see what might be revealed beneath the Icelandic skirts.

Katinka remained seated. She felt as though reborn in here, alone with Huus in the silence beneath the falling rain.

"They are not playing," she said.

"No, because of the rain."

They both listened to the falling rain.

"What a din there was, though," she said.

Katinka would have preferred to stay there and sit listening to the rain. But nevertheless she rose: "Are they really of Italy?"

"That's what he said."

She looked through one of the peepholes. "Yes," she said. "It's Italy."

There was some artificial light in there directed on the pictures, which shone out in bright colours.

"It is so beautiful."

"It's the gulf," said Huus, "near Naples."

The picture was not bad. Gulf and beach and city lay bathed in shimmering sunlight. Boats were skimming across the blue waters.

"Naples," breathed Katinka in a quiet voice.

She continued to look in the peephole. Huus looked at the same picture in the peephole alongside hers.

"Have you been there?"

"Yes, I was there for two months."

"Sailing?"

"Yes, to Sorrento."

"Sorrento," Katinka lingered over the foreign name as she gently repeated it.

"Yes," she said. "Travel."

They went along the row of peepholes and looked at the pictures while standing beside each other. The rain was less intense as it fell on the roof, and finally it was no more than a few drops.

They saw Rome and the Coliseum. Huus told her about them.

"It is so grand," said Katinka, "that it almost makes you afraid."

"I like Naples best."

Outside, the barrel organs started to play. The merry-go-round bell rang. Katinka had almost forgotten where she was.

"I don't think it's raining any longer."

"No, it's gone off now."

Katinka looked round her in the room. "Then Bai will be waiting," she said.

She went back and once more looked at the Bay of Naples with the hurrying boats.

Bai came in and said that the street was open to regular traffic again.

"So I suppose we can go out to the park?" he said.

They went. The air was cool and fresh. Crowds of happy people were making their way towards the park.

The trees and hawthorn hedges were perfumed after the rain.

The sun was sinking, and over by the entrance to the park coloured lamps were being lit on the decorated arch. The lads were drifting along with their arms around the lasses' waists. All the benches along the road were occupied by young people sitting close together, secretly courting.

"Now we're going to have a dance," said Bai.

Outside the dance floor crowds of adolescent boys and girls were watching over the railings. Inside, the dance floor resounded to the beat of a polka.

"Come on, Tik," said Bai. "We'll open the dancing."

Bai danced ferociously and continued to weave his way in and out among the other couples.

"Oh Bai, please," said Katinka, quite breathless.

"I can still manage to shuffle around," said Bai. He was swinging his hips to a completely wrong rhythm.

"Oh Bai, please."

"I can still get her going," said Bai as they went over to Huus.

"Now I'd better keep up the good work," he said, clicking his heels as at the club balls, "and get the ladies moving."

Bai was making Katinka feel uncomfortable.

"Bai is so frisky," she said when he had left them.

"Will you dance with me?" said Huus.

"Yes. In a moment. Let's just wait a moment."

They could see Bai waggling his hips together with a buxom farmer's daughter in a velvet corsage.

"Let's walk a little," said Katinka.

They left the dance floor and walked a little way down the road, where the music was not so loud.

Katinka sat down. "Sit down," she said. "This makes one so tired."

It was quiet in the woods. Only a few odd sounds of music reached them now and then. They sat in silence. Huus fiddled with a stick on the ground.

"Where is she now?" Katinka asked suddenly. She was sitting there looking down.

"She?"

"Yes, your fiancée."

"She is married, thank goodness."

"Thank goodness?"

"Yes, one would always feel some responsibility if she were now simply left high and dry."

"But you couldn't help that."

Katinka was silent for a time: "If she was fond of you."

"She was fond of me," said Huus. "I know that now."

Katinka rose. "Has she any children?" she asked. They had already moved a little further along the road.

"Yes, a little boy."

They spoke no more until they reached the dance floor. "Shall we dance now?" said Katinka.

The small lanterns had been lit all around and threw a sparse light down on the benches along the sides. The couples danced out into the light and then back again into the darkness; everything on the dance floor constituted a black, indeterminate, rather restless throng gliding in and out.

Huus and Katinka started to dance. Huus danced calmly and led confidently, and for Katinka it was as though she was at rest in his arms.

She heard it all, music and voices and tramping, as something quite far away and was only aware that he led her so confidently, in and out.

Huus continued to dance in the same quiet way. Katinka felt her heart beating and knew that her cheeks were burning. But she did not ask him to stop and she said nothing.

They continued to dance.

"Can we see the sky?" said Katinka suddenly.

"No," said Huus. "The trees are hiding it."

"So the trees are hiding it," whispered Katinka.

They danced.

"Huus," she said, looking up at him and not knowing why her eyes were full of tears, "I'm tired."

Huus stopped and protected her with his arm as they made their way through the throng.

"This is great fun," said Bai. He whirled past them at the entrance.

They went down the step and drifted out along a path.

It was quite dark among the trees; it was as though it had grown hotter again after the rain, and they were met by the intense perfume of flowering hawthorn.

All around beneath trees and in the undergrowth there was whispering and movement as tightly embracing couples hid on the benches in the darkness.

"Huus, Bai must be waiting for us," said Katinka. "We'd better go."

They turned back.

"Aye," said Bai, "let's go and see what all the screeching is about over there. There are supposed to be some 'chorus girls' in the pavilion, and they're said to be rather nice to look at. But first I'm going to have a last dance with that little country lass over there. You go and shake a leg with Katinka again, Huus, and make sure she doesn't just sit there."

Huus put his arm round Katinka, and they danced again.

Katinka was oblivious as to whether they had danced for a minute or an hour as they walked through the woods in the direction of the pavilion.

Five ladies were singing at the door to greet them. They were waving tassels and placed two fingers on their hearts:

"Here come we,
Jolly good company,
Fighting as you see,
All male tyranny…"

"There's a cosy corner here," said Bai. "We can see the ladies from here."

They sat down. It was almost impossible to see faces around them for smoke and fumes. The five ladies were singing about bayonets and bravery. When they had finished, they drank some punch and flirted with their onlookers by putting rose petals in their bodices and giggling behind their grubby fans.

"Nice girls," said Bai.

Katinka scarcely heard him; Huus sat with his head in his hands, staring down at the dirty floor.

A little pianist looking like a grasshopper threw himself at a piano as though he was going to play it with his thin nose.

The ladies argued as to whose turn it was.

"It's you, Julie," came an irate whisper from behind the fans. "God knows. It's Julie."

"The Chimney Sweep," Julie addressed the crowd in a loud voice.

"That's not allowed," shouted a couple of ladies behind their fans down to the pianist. "She's singing a song that's not allowed, Sørensen."

Down in the hall people started tapping their glasses.

"Ugh, just because Josefine can't sing it."

Miss Julie sang, "The Chimney Sweep":

"Our August, the chimney sweep
A splendid coat of arms did keep…"

Bai thumped the table so hard he almost broke the toddy glasses:

"How's that, Tik?" he said.

Katinka started. She had not been listening at all.

"All right," she said.

"Brilliant," said Bai, "brilliant." He clapped again.

"The popular ballad singer, Miss Mathilde Nielsen," shouted Miss Julie.

The popular ballad singer Miss Mathilde Nielsen wore a long dress and was solemn in appearance. The other ladies said, "Mathilde's got some voice." Mathilde had fallen and split her nose as a child.

While the piano introduction was being played, she placed her hand on her heart.

It was the song about Sorrento.

"There the tall and darkling pines
Give their shade to farmers' vines

There orange grove and luscious lime
Their perfumes give to this sweet clime;
There boats rock gently by the shore
As happy lovers by the score
So loud Madonna's praises sing
And then to her their prayers do bring."

Miss Mathilde Nielsen's singing was sentimental with long, tremulous notes.

When the song was at an end, the 'ladies' applauded by striking their fans against their outstretched hands.

The singer of popular ballads, 'Miss' Nielsen, bowed to express her thanks.

"I do believe that song's got Tik blubbering," said Bai. Katinka really had tears in her eyes as she sat there.

They went outside. "Let's go back through the churchyard," said Bai.

"Through the churchyard?" said Katinka.

"Aye, it's the shortest way and it's rather nice."

Katinka took Huus' arm and they followed Bai. They emerged from the woods and walked down an avenue. Noise and music died away behind them.

"Aye," said Bai, "quite a day, a day put to good use." He went on about the dance: "They do go at it, those village kids. And the 'ladies'. 'Miss Julie', some girl in those boots, bright lass. And Marie, well now we'll see what's been going on. I know her."

The other two said nothing. Nor was either of them listening. It was so quiet that they could hear their own steps on the ground. At the end of the avenue, the iron gate leading into the churchyard towered up with its great cross above.

"Oh, but Bai," said Katinka.

"Do you think there are ghosts in here?" said Bai. He opened the side gate.

They went in. Katinka took Huus' arm as they entered through the gate. The churchyard looked like a great garden in the dusk. Roses and box hedges and jasmines and limes filled the air with a heavy scent, and grey and white stones rose among the hedges.

Katinka held tight onto Huus' arm as they walked along.

Bai led the way. He tramped past the shrubbery and swung his arms about as though he was trying to frighten a flock of poultry.

Katinka stopped: "Just look at that."

An open space had been made through the trees, opening up the view down across the fields to the fjord. The dusk floated like a veil over the dark, shiny surface of the water, silent and dreamy.

All was silent, as though life itself had died beneath the perfumed air. They stood close to each other, quite still.

They moved on slowly. Katinka stopped now and then and quietly read the inscriptions on the stones which stood out white in the dusk. She read them, names and years, in a quiet, tremulous voice.

"Loved and missed."

"Loved beyond the grave."

"He that loveth another hath fulfilled the law."

She went closer and raised the branches of the weeping willow; she was going to read the name on the stone.

Then there was a rustling noise from behind the willow.

"Huus," she said and grabbed his arm.

Something started off and fled over the fence.

"It was a couple," said Huus.

"Oh, I was so frightened," said Katinka, holding her hands

to her breast.

She continued to walk close to him; her heart was beating fiercely.

They no longer spoke. There was a rustling in the shrubbery now and then and Katinka started.

"There, there, dear, it's all right," whispered Huus as though to a child. Katinka's hand was trembling beneath his.

Bai was standing at the end of the pathway.

"Are you there?" he said.

He opened the gate. It clicked shut on its iron hinges after them.

Out in the avenue, Bai took Huus aside:

"It's a flaming scandal," he said, "that people can behave like that. It's a desecration of sacred ground. Kjær had told me about it, of course. The things those wretches get up to. But I didn't think it was possible, damn it. Not even to have respect for the dead in a cemetery, the garden of the dead. Bloody disgrace. You can't even be left in peace on the damned benches."

Huus could have hit him.

They went down through the streets. The tents were closed and deserted. Here and there a tradesman would be gathering his wares with the help of a solitary torch.

The noise from the inn could be heard in the street. Sleepy, wilting people were drifting home in pairs.

Marie emerged at the entrance to the hotel. She was tired and worn.

Katinka waited by the carriage. People round about were hitching their horses and driving off. The 'nightingales' were singing at the tops of their voices out in the courtyard.

They took their seats. Bai wanted to drive and sat

with Marie.

"Oh my darling, oh my darling,
Oh my darling Clementine…"

"They do keep at it," said Bai.

They drove through the night, past the forest and on over the flat fields.

Marie sat there, bent over the basket on her lap. Huus and Katinka sat in silence, staring out across the countryside. Bai spoke now and then.

"Whoa."

"Come on, easy now."

And then all was silent as before.

Bai wanted "something to keep him going" and pestered Marie until she found a bottle of port wine.

"Do you want some?" he said.

"No, thank you," said Huus.

"You're making a mistake there, damn it." Bai took the bottle from his mouth. "Your stomach needs something to stand against the night air."

Bai took another gulp. "You learn that in the field," he said.

He started to talk about the Prussians and the war.

"Nice people," he said, "taken one by one. Eat a lot, eat a dreadful lot, but kind-hearted, really kind-hearted taken on their own. But when they're in the army, then they're proper devils."

No one replied. Marie was nodding again.

Katinka merely wished he would be quiet.

"But my hat, how they can stuff themselves," said Bai again.

He started to become all patriotic and spoke about old Denmark and the blood-red Danish flag. Then he lapsed into silent reflections when no one answered.

The only sound was that made by the horses in their harness. Now and again a cock was heard to crow over the fields.

"Put your shawl on," said Huus. "It's cold."

He carefully laid the blue shawl around Katinka's shoulders.

Gradually, day dawned over the fields.

"I suppose you'll give us a bit of breakfast," said Bai. They were home and standing on the steps in the grey morning light, not quite knowing what to do.

"Yes, if you like," said Katinka.

But Huus had to go home. It was the busy time of the year.

"Oh well, as you like," said Bai. He yawned and went inside. Marie had gone off laden with the baskets.

Huus and Katinka were left alone. She leant against the doorpost. They did not speak for a moment or two.

"Well, thank you for a lovely day," she said. The words came gently and uncertainly.

"Surely I'm the one who should say thank you." This came in the form of an exclamation, and in a flash Huus had taken her hand and kissed it twice and three times with burning lips.

And then he was up in the carriage and away.

"What the devil took hold of him?" said Bai, coming out. "Has he gone?"

Katinka remained standing on the same spot. "Yes," she said, "he left."

She leant on the doorpost and then quietly went inside.

Katinka sat by the open window. Day had come in all its fullness. Larks and all the birds were singing in celebration over the meadow. The summer fields were filled with song and sun and chirping.

IV

The guard dog was asleep on its chain in the hot yard and was not to be awakened. A couple of scrubbed tubs had been put out to dry in the sun.

Katinka opened the parsonage front door; all that could be heard was the buzzing of the flies in the cool light rooms.

She went in through the summerhouse and out into the garden. There was no one to be seen and all was quite silent. Balls and mallets lay abandoned on the croquet lawn. The rose bushes were drooping in the heat.

"Is it you, my dear Mrs Bai?" The words issued quietly from the summerhouse. Mrs Linde nodded: "Linde is preparing his sermon."

"They are all out in the back garden. The Kiærs came, you know, a whole crowd of them with some of their friends. And that's not really convenient when Linde is preparing a sermon."

"Are the Kiærs here?" said Katinka.

"Yes, they came for coffee. They are in the back garden along with the new doctor. And what about you? You've been to the fair. Huus told me all about it."

"Yes, it was a lovely day," said Katinka. She found it difficult to speak these words, her heart was beating so.

Old Mr Linde appeared at the garden door. He had a handkerchief on his head. The handkerchiefs came out every

Friday evening when Mr Linde started working on his sermon.

"Is it our dear Mrs Katinka," he said. "And are you well?"

The old minister came across to the summerhouse door. He wanted to hear about the fair.

Katinka scarcely knew what she was saying. While speaking she suddenly felt an indescribable longing for Huus.

"Yes, he is a really good man," said Mrs Linde after Katinka had said something or other, and Katinka blushed scarlet.

"Yes," said the old minister, "he's a nice man."

He removed the handkerchief and laid it before him on the summerhouse table. He went on asking about the fair: "It was getting on for morning before the people here came home," he said.

"They must be allowed to enjoy themselves occasionally." The old parson continued to make the odd comment, and Katinka replied without having understood a word of what he had said.

"Linde, my dear – what about your sermon?"

"Yes, dear. Yes, Mrs Bai," he said. "It's Saturday evening already."

The old minister shambled away with his handkerchief in his hand.

"Would you not like to go down to the others, Mrs Bai?" said Mrs Linde.

"Are you sure I cannot help you with anything?"

"No, thank you. I'm only going to give them what I have ready, a few peas and some ham."

Katinka rose.

"Go through the courtyard," said Mrs Linde.

Katinka had not seen Huus for the three days since the fair, during which time she had both waited and hoped. And feared what she was hoping. Now she was to see him again.

Laughter and noise from the back garden could be heard far out across the meadow. Katinka opened the gate and went in.

"There's our lovely lady," shouted Agnes. They were playing odd man out on the big lawn.

Katinka had only seen Huus, standing there in the middle of the group. How pale and sad he looked.

It struck Katinka that perhaps he had been unable to sleep, just as she had. And she smiled nervously at him, with her head bent like that of a young girl.

Agnes joined her, and they came to stand in front of Huus.

"Oh, come on," said Agnes to Huus, "We know what's wrong: you've had a hangover of course. And so no one has set eyes on you for three days."

"And we have missed you."

"Mrs Bai wouldn't let us have our coffee yesterday because we were to wait for you."

Katinka turned her eyes down to the ground, but she made no effort to stop Agnes. She felt as though it was she herself who was saying how she had been waiting for him.

"And what sort of a way is this to behave when one is supposed to be responsible for a couple of chicks?" said Agnes.

The other two said not a word. But Katinka felt Huus looking at her, and she stood there with her head bowed before him.

They went on to play postman's knock. He was all she saw. They only exchanged the words of the game in low voices. Neither of them would have been able to speak aloud in a normal voice.

Katinka did not realise that in the game her hands were lingering in his and only reluctantly releasing them.

The table was to be laid for supper in the summerhouse. The old minister and Mr Andersen came with Louise and

Little Miss Jensen.

"Well," said Agnes, "we were allowed to have a smell of the ham at last."

Before going to table, Louise had already been skipping in front of the new doctor and displaying her 'beauty'.

When they were all seated in the summerhouse, old Mr Linde called in through the door to ask whether a couple out on the lovers' bench had not been forgotten. The 'lovers' bench' was an old mouldering bench between two trees down by the pond.

"It is so lovely and dark there," said Mrs Linde. "In the old days, when our sons were courting, there was always a couple that emerged from there, that's to say each on their own side of the summerhouse here. Aye, in those days…"

The 'lovers' bench' was Mrs Linde's favourite subject.

"Aye, Linde, some people have been very happy."

She started to count up all the people who had become engaged in the parsonage. So-and-so and so-and-so… It turned into a happy conversation across the entire table about all that courting and all those engagements.

"Yes, there was that summer when both Rikard and Hans Beck got engaged."

"Agnes knew of course; she had always rattled the catches before opening the doors."

"And then the path through the hazels."

"Of course, there was always the risk of disturbing someone."

"You could always hear the rustling through the branches as someone ran off."

"Miss Horten had a horrid yellow skirt. It simply shone."

"Yes," said the old minister, "you have to be careful of gaudy colours."

"Oh, but it's so lovely in the hazel walk," exclaimed one girl.

At this, people laughed so loudly they leant over the table.

"Linde, Linde," shouts Mrs Linde. "Remember it's Saturday." The old parson is laughing so much he starts coughing.

"But it really was as though you could always hear kissing in all the corners.

"Yes," says Mrs Linde, adopting a practical attitude, "they have all done very well."

"Your health, dear Mrs Katinka, let us drink to each other," says the old parson.

Katinka started: "Thank you…"

The conversation turned on one couple, the last one on the lovers' bench. They had a little boy already.

"Was it a boy they got?"

"Yes, a lovely boy."

"He weighed eight pounds," said Mrs Linde.

"And they have their own home."

"All in no time."

"And all this billing and cooing. You would think they were still on their honeymoon."

They had finished eating, and Mrs Linde made a sign to the minister.

"Aye, aye," said the old parson. "Shall we drink to mother, then?"

"That was a lovely meal. Thank you so much."

Everyone rose, and there was the buzz of voices out in the garden. Katinka leant against the wall. It was as though all noise and talk out there was so far away and she saw nothing but Huus' pale, expressive face, that beloved face of his.

A couple of maids came to clear the table, and Katinka went out into the garden. They were going to play hide and seek. Agnes had already started counting.

The old parson wished them all good night. It was Saturday, he said. He met Bai up by the gate: "Good evening, stationmaster. I'm afraid I must think about my sermon."

Louise was standing by the big jasmine bush. People were rushing around and hiding behind bushes all over the place.

"She's peeping, she's peeping," someone shouted as they rushed past the jasmine bush.

And then there was silence.

"I'm coming."

Katinka went into the summerhouse. She closed the door behind her; she was so tired. And all the words spoken at the table had as it were settled on her like some great pain against which there was no help.

She sat quietly on her own when the door was opened and closed:

"Huus!"

"Katinka. Oh dear Katinka." It was a voice in despair and in tears, and he grabbed her hands and kissed and kissed them as he knelt at her feet.

"Yes, my dear. Yes, my dear."

Katinka freed her hands and supported herself on his shoulder for a moment as he knelt there: "Yes, Huus, yes."

The tears were running down her cheeks. With indescribable tenderness he let his hand glide down through the sobbing woman's hair.

"Oh, dearest Huus, time will soothe all this. You… when you…" She removed his hand from her hair and supported herself on the table: "When you leave and we see each other no more."

"Not see each other ever again?"

"No, Huus. It must be so. But I will always remember you,

As Trains Pass By

always and forever."

She spoke so gently and with a thousand sorrowful caresses in her voice. "Katinka," said Huus. He raised his face to her, and it was bathed in tears.

Katinka looked down on his face, where she loved every feature. His eyes, his mouth, his forehead, which she was never to see again; never to be close to him.

She took a step as though to go. Then she turned round towards Huus, who was standing by the table.

"Kiss me," she said, putting her head onto his chest.

He took her head between his hands and whispered her name all the time between his kisses.

Out in the garden they were rushing around all over the place. Louise flew through the hazel walk after the new doctor, almost overturning Bai at the end of the path.

"Aye, we were at the fair," said Bai. "Nice day. Saw a couple of nice girls in the woods, smart girls in boots. A real breath of fresh air, Kiær, old boy."

"So Huus said," says Kiær.

"Huus." Bai stops and lowers his voice. "Huus. What did I say? That man doesn't know anything at all about women. He just sat there like a skinned chicken watching the 'nightingales'. It was a sorry sight, Kiær, pitiful to see in a well-built man."

Louise turned up on the new doctor's arm, up by the jasmine bush.

It was beginning to grow dusk. Couples were drifting around here and there in the garden. A name was called out from down in the hazel walk: "Yes," came the reply from down by the pond.

And then, while the Saturday evening bells were ringing, everything grew quieter. Folk moved silently in the direction of the big grassy bank, exchanging brief, quiet remarks.

Katinka sat beside Agnes. The parson's daughter always made a fuss of 'our lovely lady'.

"Sing a little, Miss Emma," said Agnes.

A little lady started to sing while they were sitting around the turf seat. It was the ballad telling how Sir Peter cast a spell of runes on Spange, the narrow bridge his beloved was to cross, in order to capture her affection. All the girls joined in the refrain.

Agnes rocked the lovely lady gently to and fro as she sang:

> "Fairest words
> Give but brief cheer
> Fairest words
> Can change our bliss to tears
> Fairest words."

And all became still again.

They sang song after song, first a single voice and then others would join in.

Katinka stayed with Agnes, silent and close to her.

"Join in the singing, lovely lady," said Agnes, bending her face down towards Katinka.

Evening was really upon them now. The bushes round about stood there like great shadows. And after the hot day, the air was fresh with dew and filled with scent.

One man spoke to Huus, and he replied. Katinka could hear his voice.

" 'Marianna' is such a nice song," said Miss Emma.

"Yes, sing 'Marianna'."

Agnes and Miss Emma sang. "Do stay where you are," said Agnes to Katinka.

"Beneath the grassy grave is sleeping
Our poor Marianna
Come gather, girls, and join in weeping.
Our poor Marianna.

The snake around her heart was twisted
And peace on earth no more existed.
Our poor Marianna."

"Is our lovely lady cold?"
"I suppose we had better be going home," said Katinka.
She rose. "I think it must be getting late," she said.

They had left the garden. She had said goodbye to him.

She had seen his face, sorrowful and pale as he quickly bowed to her. She had felt his hand as he shook hers, so desperately that it hurt, and heard Bai's:

"Bye, Huus. We'll see you before long."

And quickly, as she forced herself to laugh at something she had not heard, she shook hands all round; and Agnes put her arm round her and ran with her up to the garden gate.

It clicked twice and closed.

And behind them they were still singing.

"Let's go this way," she said. It was a path across the meadows, along the parsonage garden; they had to go in single file.

Katinka walked slowly behind Bai.

"Good night." The leave-takings floated over to them. Old Linde had gone up onto his mound. He was waving his handkerchief.

"Good night, parson."

"Good night."

They went on across the meadow. The parson's 'Good night' had suddenly brought the tears to Katinka's eyes, and she continued to weep silently. She turned around twice and looked back at Linde standing on his mound.

"Are you coming?" said Bai.

They arrived home.

Bai checked the track and chatted as he fiddled about and finally settled down. And she went around and did all the everyday things, covering the furniture and watering the plants and closing the doors.

It was all as though through a veil, as though she were dreaming.

She rose the following day and set about all her customary tasks. The ten o'clock train came and went and she sat at the window looking out across the meadows, which lay there as they had done yesterday.

She talked; she was asked about everyday things and gave everyday answers. She went into the kitchen to help Marie.

Windows and doors were open. The bells started ringing from the chapel.

Marie was in the midst of a long conversation when her mistress said, "I'm going to church."

And she was gone before Marie managed to say anything.

It was almost as though her mistress ran across the sun-drenched meadows.

V

A couple of days later, Katinka went "home".

One of her brothers had a grocer's shop in the town where she was born, and she went to stay with him. The other brothers were scattered all over the place.

Her sister-in-law was a nice little woman who brought a child into the world each year and toddled around half embarrassed and anxious in her everlasting pregnancy. She had become very indolent and rather slow. She was not able to do much apart from giving birth and nursing.

In the house there was always one of the rooms in which they had not managed to hang the curtains. They all lay there, clean and starched, spread out over all the chairs, waiting. There was always washing to be done for all those little ones; short lines of drying linen and socks were fixed everywhere. Food was never ready in time for meals and there were never enough plates when the family was finally seated at table.

"Little Mi and mother will share this plate," said the little woman.

There was a constant banging of doors and every half hour a screech like that of a stuck pig resounded through the house. It was one of the little ones falling down somewhere or other in one of the corners. They were always covered in bumps and bruises.

"Oh," said Katinka's brother. "There we go again."

"Aye, what am I to do, Kristoffer?" said the little woman.

She was always saying, "Aye, what am I to do, Kristoffer?" and looking helpless.

Katinka gradually introduced some peace and quiet into the house. She needed to have something to do; she needed to know that she was useful, and she went around ever so quietly while everything was seen to.

Her little sister-in-law sat there relieved and smiling gratefully from her chair in one of the corners. She always sat in the corners, behind a bureau or beside the sofa, with a timid smile on her face.

Katinka preferred to stay indoors while she was there. The old furniture from her home was all there along with all the other old things. Her father's masterpiece, the oak cupboard with the carved figures on the doors had stood in the drawing room at home, in the middle of the wall between the windows.

"It's Moses and his prophets," said her father. Katinka thought that "those men" were the most wonderful things in the world.

And the marble table that had been bought at an auction and on which the "best" things were symmetrically arranged in rows: the silver sugar bowl and the jug and the silver cup that had been given as a mark of special esteem by the guild.

As she went round tidying the house, Katinka kept finding memories from home – an old, inscribed cup, a yellowing picture, three or four plates.

The old plates with the blue Chinaman and the garden with the three trees and the little bridge over the brook. What a lot of tales they had told each other about those Chinese figures, at home on Sundays when they were using their best plates.

Katinka asked if she might keep the old plates.

"Keep them?" said the little woman. "Oh, heavens above,

they are all chipped." Everything in the house was chipped! "Everything gets spoilt here. But what am I to do?"

So Katinka preferred to stay indoors, or else she would go up to visit the grave in the churchyard. It was best up there. She often felt like a widow sitting by her husband's grave. He had died so soon; they had had such a short time together, and now she was alone, quite alone.

As she sat there, she read the inscription on the gravestone, the names of her mother and father.

Did they love each other? Her father, who was forever grumbling, sitting there to be waited on. And her mother, who had been completely transformed after his death, as though she had suddenly blossomed out again.

How little she had really known her parents.

But how little they knew each other, all these people living and moving alongside each other.

Katinka leant her head against the trunk of the weeping willow. She was overcome by a sense of bitterness and sadness such as she had never known before.

She rarely went out into the streets or into town. There were so many new things everywhere, and everything was different from those days. Nothing but new faces and new names, people who were strangers to her.

She had been over to take a look at the old house. Some back rooms had been built onto the old workshop. And there were new windows and new doors, and their old dovecote had been turned into a gable room.

Katinka no longer went into the old courtyard.

She had met Thora Berg in the street.

"But surely…" yes, it was the same old voice, "that's Katinka."

"Yes."

"Good heavens, girl, what are you doing here? And you've not changed at all."

"Nor have you," said Katinka. She had tears in her eyes.

"I? Good Lord, I live here now of course. Since the spring. We were moved here."

"Yes, my dear, a lot of water has flowed under the bridge. I suppose you don't have any children?"

"No."

"I thought not. You just thank God for that, my dear. I have four. And five more boarders. No, you don't get far on the second senior captain's pay. But what about you? Where do you live, all of you? Still in the same place? Good Lord! When you are in the army you don't live in the same place for long at a time."

Thora continued to talk. Katinka walked beside her and looked at her. It was really the same face, but it had as it were grown more severe in appearance, and then it was yellowish and pointed at the chin.

"You're looking at me, my girl," said Thora. "No, let me tell you, living isn't all a string of club dances."

She said she would come and see her and then take her home with her to the nest.

"But it's revision time, you know – and we're up to our eyes in French verbs."

They parted. Katinka stood there and watched her go. She was wearing a short, skimpy velvet jacket over a yellow dress. It was all chosen at random and looked as though it was a little too tight.

It was not until about a week later that they saw each other again at church.

"Do I ever get out? Yes, and I've been wanting to come and find you every day," said Thora. "Come and see us on

Wednesday. Wednesday about three o'clock. Wednesday's the day there's most peace and quiet," she said.

Katinka was there that Wednesday.

Thora was in the kitchen when she arrived, and Katinka waited in the living room. This room was too big for the furniture in it, furniture that Thora had been given on marrying and which was now pale and faded; the pieces stood there and seemed to be stretching out in an effort to reach each other along the wall. By the window there was a modern flower stand containing a rubber plant alongside a cane chair on an embroidered rug. These were the choice items.

On the table there lay a few collections of poems in faded bindings along with a couple of panoramas of the Rhine, souvenirs from Thora's honeymoon with her captain.

On high walls papered in yellow there hung some paintings of flowers in narrow gilt frames. They represented roses and pansies with big drops of dew that looked like glass beads scattered over their leaves. Katinka knew them, Thora had painted them when she was a girl.

"Yes, one uses all one's old talents to decorate the place," said Thora, coming in as Katinka stood there looking at the roses and the glass beads.

The captain opened the door, dressed in a denim jacket and collar and tie, "Is dinner ready?" he asked.

"We have a visitor, Dahl," said Thora. And the door closed. "Dahl is drawing a map, you see," she said.

The captain appeared again wearing his off-duty uniform jacket. "How nice, how nice," he said, starting to walk up and down the floor. When the captain was not drawing maps or commanding his troops, he always had a payment date and a complicated piece of arithmetic in his head. These were left over from his days as a lieutenant and the honeymoon with the two panoramic views of the Rhine.

Thora sat there and talked and talked. Katinka was struck by how restless her eyes had become, moving first to the door and then to Dahl, talking incessantly the while.

"It's quarter past," said the captain.

"The boys aren't here yet," said Thora.

"So we can't have our meal," said the captain. "You must realise, Mrs Bai, that it is the boys who are the bosses in this house."

Thora said nothing. The captain sat down on a chair over by the writing desk. The back fell off it.

"It's about time we had that chair repaired," he said.

"Yes, Dahl."

"We've been going to have it done for the past six months, Mrs Bai," said the captain. He inclined a little in her direction. "That is the customary state of affairs in this house."

The boys came charging down the stairs from the attic like wild animals being chased.

"There they are," said Thora. They went into the dining room. The captain had offered Katinka his arm; Thora quietly put the fallen chair back in place, supporting it on the wall.

"Where have you been?" said the captain.

"We've been bathing," said the boys. They had been smoking for an hour by the roadside and then put their heads into a bowl of water.

"These are mine," said Thora. And by mine she meant a nine-year-old boy and three small straight-haired girls.

The captain had bicarbonate of soda on his food and after each mouthful he wiped his Napoleonic beard, which was waxed and carefully tended to adorn his weary face.

The captain talked about wage conditions on the railways.

The boys were five upper-class puppies, pupils in the lower

secondary school. They called 'my four' the paupers and regularly debagged the nine-year-old but were otherwise quite good-natured.

They ate like wolves and said they were never full except when they were "at home at the hall".

The nine-year-old sat there with big, old-fashioned eyes, looking from the boys to Thora.

"The porcelain is chipped in honour of visitors," said the captain. He handed Katinka the cucumber salad in a chipped dish.

"Oh, it happens so easily, captain," said Katinka.

One of the boys continued to ask in a low voice for more potatoes; he had seen there were no more in the dish.

"There are cucumbers," said Thora. "Would you like some more, Dahl?"

"You are not getting anything yourself," said Katinka. "We have plenty, dear."

"My dear Mrs Bai," said the captain, "It is her pleasure. In this house we know nothing of that luxury called peace and quiet."

Thora cut the meat for the smallest of the straight-haired girls.

"As you can hear, the captain is in such a good mood today," she said with a laugh. "Isn't that right, captain?"

The captain was always in that mood.

"What did Gustav get for geography?"

"Could do better," came the reply in a low voice from a plate.

"Do you think your father will be satisfied with that, Gustav?"

"Father doesn't care," replied the low voice.

They rose from the table. All the doors in the house were

slammed after the boys.

"Aye, Mrs Bai," said the captain, "those are Thora's invading forces."

"She is afraid that we might have peace and quiet in the house one day."

The captain returned to his maps. Thora rummaged through all kinds of coffee blends behind the coffee maker.

"Can't I help you?" said Katinka.

"Thank you, dear."

Thora had acquired red blotches in her cheeks and she put her hands up to her temples: "There's always rather a lot about dinner time," she said.

"But you get too worked up over it, Thora," said Katinka, who was herself quite flushed.

"When you have all that nonsense from morning to evening, my dear," said Thora.

She was not left in peace at her sewing table. The doors were opening and shutting all the time. The boys had sworn that they were not going to have that "chat over coffee" and every other minute they rushed up and down the stairs from the loft to ask about words.

Thora held her hand to her forehead and went from English to German.

The nine-year-old was "practising" in the dining room.

"Nikolai, must you always practise when I've got a headache. Do stop."

Nikolai tiptoed quietly away from the piano. Thora always grumbled at her 'own' when she had been tormented by these boys who were always hungry.

Thora sat down on the sofa in the corner and curled up her legs as she had so often done as a girl.

They talked about people in the town.

"Yes, they are all new families; the old ones have gone."

"Yes, the old ones have gone," said Katinka. She looked at Thora, who had leant her head against the back of the sofa and closed her eyes. How sunken those eyes had become.

"Your brother is about the only one of the old ones left," said Thora.

"Oh, there must be a few."

Thora laughed: "Good Lord, your poor sister-in-law," she said. "Is she really on the way again?"

"Yes, poor thing."

They sat for a while. Then Thora opened her eyes and said, "Yes, my dear, we are all here for the propagation of the species."

Thora closed her eyes, and the two friends sat in silence.

"Yes," Thora said again, "life's a strange thing."

Katinka did not stay to tea. She said she had promised to go home. She needed to get out into the fresh air and to be alone. When she was down in the street, the idea came to her that she might go and visit her old teacher. It was so quiet near the old woman's home, so unchanged. Katinka turned down the street in which she lived. Tears came to her eyes when she saw the three green lime trees outside the windows. And besides, she had not been far from tears all the time she had spent at Thora's.

She mounted the few steps above the green basement entrance and knocked. A scent of roses and summer apples met her when the door opened.

The old teacher was fiddling about with rose petals spread out on newspaper on the bed, ready to be made into potpourri.

"And the people from Holmstrup had been there, all the young girls."

"They want their berries from the tree," she says. "It's just

126

about finished now."

Katinka had to go out to look at the tree and "her" roses.

There had just been three roses for Mrs Bystrøm's wreath, indeed there really had been only three roses.

They went inside again. The old teacher went on chatting as she moved to and fro, so that her words were lost between the doors. Katinka sat on the raised area by the window, just now and again saying yes or no. Through the open kitchen door there was a view across the green garden; the birds were chirping so loud as to be heard indoors.

How quiet it was here, as though there was no other world.

Katinka looked at the old pictures, faded in their skewed frames; she knew every one of them. The silver coffee pot on the table, the showpiece with its three exquisite cups and saucers and on the consol, before the greying mirror, the fine pieces of bric-a-brac with handkerchiefs spread over them, and the mats on the floor in front of all the doors, and the cats purring on their cushions.

She knew it all.

The old teacher went on chattering and going in and out. Katinka was no longer listening. It was beginning to grow dark in this room, shaded by the lime trees and with the old corners half in darkness.

It was the second time the old teacher mentioned Huus' name from out in the kitchen. Katinka started. She thought she had said it herself, lost in thought.

"There's a Mr Huus out your way," the teacher said again.

"Yes, Huus the bailiff," said Katinka. "Do you know him?"

The old teacher appeared in the doorway. Indeed she knew him. He was second cousin to her own cousin Karl from Kærsholm.

"The Kærsholms who were married to two generations of

the Lundgaards."

And she started talking about Huus and his mother, who was a Lundgaard, one of the Lundgaards from Falster, and about their farm and about his relatives and about cousin Karl from Kærsholm and the whole family as she walked back and forth.

She lit some candles in the kitchen and occupied herself with the roses on the bed in the bedroom. Katinka sat silently in her corner and heard only his name recurring time and time again.

It was the first time she had heard his name in all those weeks.

"But what sort of a person is he?" said the old teacher. She came in, lifted the sleeping cat off the armchair and sat down a little way from the window with her hands folded over the cat on her lap.

Katinka started to talk, a few unremarkable words, hesitantly, and as though she was thinking of something else. But then she was swept away: talking about him, mentioning his name, being able to mention his name.

And she told all about Christmas and the blue shawl and New Year's Eve, when he arrived in the sleigh and the winter's nights when they had walked some way with him under all those stars.

"Yes," said the old teacher from her chair, "they are nice people, the Huus'."

Katinka went on talking in a low voice through the dusk, from her corner.

How he had helped her in the garden when spring came; he had planted the roses for her; there was no limit to what he was able to do.

"Yes," said the old teacher, "they are a nice family."

And the summer days that came, and the fair. She told about it all.

The old teacher had started nodding in her chair. She was inclined to become sleepy when she had to listen, and before long she was asleep with her hands folded over her cat.

Katinka stopped talking and sat in silence. The gas lamps were lit outside, illuminating the sitting room: the pictures on the walls, the old clock and the old teacher sitting with her cat on her lap and her head down on her breast.

The old teacher awoke and raised her head.

"Yes," she said, "he is a nice person."

Katinka did not hear what she said. She rose simply in order to leave and to get away. And out in the fresh air, along the roads circling the town, as she walked it was as though her longing increased with every step.

A couple of days later, she received a letter from Bai. The most remarkable thing here, he wrote, concerns Huus. He went to Copenhagen last week on business, as he said. And what do you think? A few days later he wrote to Kiær asking to be released from his job. He had been given the opportunity of going to Holland and Belgium, he wrote, just fancy, on a scholarship, and he would send a replacement, and this replacement arrived yesterday. Kiær is furious and I'm sorry as well now as we had got so used to the dry old stick.

The letter lay open on the table in front of Katinka. And she had read it again and again: she had not known that she was still hoping. But she had thought that it was all nothing but a dream: a miracle must happen. But she had to see him again, and he would not leave.

But now he had left. He had left and gone away.

Her nephews were jabbering away around her as they ate

their milk sops:

"Auntie, Auntie Tik."

The smallest but one fell off his chair and let out a howl.

"Oh dear, did Emil fall and hurt himself?" said the little wife.

Katinka lifted Emil up and wiped his face and, without realising it, returned to her letter.

Left and gone away.

But now she wanted to go home, to be in her own surroundings and not among these strangers.

At least she would be at home.

It was her last afternoon there. The nursemaid had gone to the plantation with the children.

Katinka and her sister-in-law were alone in the sitting room. The sister-in-law was brooding over her baby clothes.

Then, just as they were sitting there, the little woman bent her head over her sewing box and sobbed.

"Oh Marie," said Katinka, "my dear Marie, what is it?"

She rose and went across to her sister-in-law. "What is it, Marie?" she said.

The little woman continued to sob with her head bent over her workbox.

Katinka placed her hands on her head and spoke quietly to her. "But, dearest Marie – dear Marie."

The little woman looked up: "Yes," she said, "you are leaving now. And you have been so kind to me."

She sobbed and again lowered her head over the workbox. "So kind to me – and here am I, simply always in this mess. Always."

Katinka was touched. She knelt down on the floor in front of the little woman and took her hands. "But Marie," she said, "things will change, you know."

"Yes," and the little woman went on weeping with her head against her, "when I'm old one day, or when I'm dead."

Katinka took her sister-in-law's hands from her face and made to speak.

But then she saw the other's child-like face, wet with tears, and the poor little misshapen body, and quietly returned to her seat, while the little woman continued to weep.

That evening, Katinka went up to the churchyard. She wanted to pay a final visit to her parents' grave.

She met Thora, who had brought a wreath up to her mother's grave; it was to mark her birthday.

The two friends stood together by the burial place.

"Aye," said Thora. "We shall lie down there one day."

They parted by Katinka's parents' grave.

"We always meet again in this world," said Thora.

Katinka went over to the grave and sat down on the bench beneath the willow. She looked at the dead stone with the lettering on it and she thought she had lost everything in this world including the place where she had been at home as a child.

What had become of it all? Everything was grey and anguished and miserable, everything.

She pictured Thora with those restless eyes of hers, and she heard the captain's remark, "The porcelain is chipped in honour of visitors," and she saw her little sister-in-law's face as she wept.

And here at this spot with its dead stone and the two names on it. This was all she had with which to remember her youth and her home.

She sat there for a long time. And she considered the life she was to live now, and it was as though it all closed over her, everything, just one single, unimaginable sense of all-engulfing hopelessness.

She alighted from the carriage onto the platform, and she allowed Bai to kiss her, and Marie took her things, and she had one thought only: to get inside, to get indoors.

It seemed to her that Huus must be in there waiting for her.

And she went ahead and opened the door to the sitting room, which stood there clean and elegant; to the bedroom; to the kitchen, where everything was shining; spotless and empty.

"Good Lord, you do look bad," were Marie's first words as she struggled with the luggage.

And then, while Katinka, pale and weary, slumped down on a chair, she started relating news about the entire district. About what had happened and what had been said. They had had summer visitors over in the inn, people who had brought their own bedstead and everything, and the parsonage had been filled to the rafters with visitors.

And then there was Huus, who had gone away all of a sudden.

"Aye, I suspected it. 'Cos he was down here on his last evening, and it felt to me just as though he was saying goodbye to it all. He sat in the sitting room all alone, and then out in the garden and here on the steps near the pigeons."

"When did he leave?" asked Katinka.

"I suppose it must be about a fortnight ago."

A fortnight.

Katinka rose quietly and went out into the garden. She walked round on the path, over to the roses, down beneath the elder. This was where he had come to say goodbye to her. She visited every spot, every single spot. She shed no tears. She felt it almost as though it was some silent ceremony.

There came a happy shout from the road. She heard Agnes' voice in the midst of the crowd. She almost started: she did not want to see them all straight away.

Agnes rushed across to welcome her almost in the manner of some big dog and nearly knocked her over; and the entire company from the parsonage arrived to be given chocolate, and a table was laid in the garden beneath the elder and they all stayed there until the eight o'clock train came.

The train chugged off and they had gone again; the noise they made could be heard as they walked along the road. Peter the porter had put the milk churns in place, and Katinka sat on the platform alone.

"Aye," said Bai from the window: "Huus sent his love."

"Thank you."

"Hmm, the days are drawing in. And there's a damn cold wind. You should come inside."

"Yes, I'm coming."

Bai closed the window.

The sound of the party from the parsonage died away. All was quiet and desolate.

Katinka sat there looking out across the darkening, silent fields. This was where she was to live now.

Ida had been writing about it in all her letters for the past month. But Mrs Abel had not dared to hope. Ida was so sanguine.

Now, with the letter in her hand, she sat howling on the wet floor cloth beside the stove.

Louise had gone for a walk, looking for mushrooms near the doctor's residence. When she came home, her mother was still rocking to and fro on the chair in the kitchen.

"What's wrong?" said Louise. She thought her mother looked very strange as she sat there.

"Ida, my youngest child," the widowed mother sobbed and started to howl again.

"Rubbish," said Louise. Her mother handed her the letter with a gesture like that of the heroic mother in some tragedy.

Louise read it dispassionately. "That's nice," she said, "for her."

"She's had a whole summer, of course."

Louise went inside and started banging on the piano. Then, as she sat there, she also started to wail with her head bent down over the keys.

"I suppose you'll send her our congratulations," she suddenly said amidst all her sobbing.

"What do you say?"

"I said I suppose you'll send our congratulations," said Louise, drying her eyes. She was starting to adapt to the new situation.

"Yes, dear," said the widowed mother in a feeble voice.

"I can take the telegram down. I'll go to the parsonage, and you can go to the Jensen's and the Miller's." Louise was organising the campaign. She understood that she was at least the sister-in-law.

She became quite child-like and shouted "Long live the post office" as she hurried away from the station, swinging her parasol in the air.

He worked for the post office.

Her mother went happily from the Jensen's to the Miller's and wept at the thought that she was now going to lose her darling child.

"Joakim Barner – one of the distinguished Barner family," said the widow. He has a place with the post office.

The mother was at the parsonage when her elder daughter arrived there.

"Yes, I felt the need to tell our spiritual adviser myself at such a solemn moment," said Mrs Abel, again making use of her handkerchief.

The old minister slapped his stomach in delight. The strawberry liqueur was put on the table together with some biscuits. Mrs Linde sat on the sofa together with Mrs Abel so as to hear how it had "come about". It had "come about" in a summerhouse down by the shore.

The old minister toasted the elder daughter Louise.

"Aye, aye, we know what happens when things start moving. One thing leads to another," said the old parson.

"Yes, Mr Linde, but the thought of losing both of them. My younger daughter..." And the widowed lady had an attack of dreadfully tender feelings for her younger daughter.

That younger daughter was as gentle as a baby foal in view of the occasion.

"Well, there is a chance she might still turn out quite nice," said Mrs Linde as she collected the cake plates after they had gone. "They're all right at bottom, Linde."

"Heaven knows what Agnes will say."

Agnes was out in the forest with some young friends.

"Oh well, thank God for that," she said on arriving home and hearing it.

"Heaven preserve us, they're going to crush the poor man to death," said Agnes standing at the platform gate watching the Abel family, who had gone to meet the son-in-law.

The little man was being swept around among the members of the Abel family as helpless as a bean in a coffee mill.

"Hmm," said Agnes, "one look is enough to tell you there's not very much to him."

She put her arm round Katinka's waist, and they went out

into the garden.

"Well," she said as she closed the gate, "they are 'so happy' now."

They sat down beneath the elder tree. Suddenly Agnes said, "I'm leaving. Next week. I've told them at home."

"I can't stand this any longer." Agnes tore to bits the leaves that had fallen on the table. "I've got to put an end to it some time."

Katinka sat staring into space. "Do you think, Agnes, that it's possible to escape sorrow by going away?" she said quietly.

"I'll get some work. I'll qualify as a teacher. There's nothing else for it. Sitting behind a glass partition in a post office would be going a bit too far. And it's too late to do anything interesting."

Katinka nodded. "Yes," she said, "that is true."

"Hmm," said Agnes. "We 'women' don't really have many chances; for the first twenty-five years of our lives we dance around waiting to get married, and for the last twenty-five we sit around waiting to be buried."

Agnes put her elbows on the table and supported her head on her hands.

"Wonderful," she breathed.

Suddenly, she put her hands to her face and burst into tears.

"And how we will eat our hearts out then," she said.

She wept for a long time with her face in her hands. Then she dropped her arms on the table. She looked at Katinka; the lovely lady sat leaning forward with her hands on her lap; slowly, the tears ran down her cheeks.

"How kind you are," said Agnes, reaching across to her. "Lovely lady."

The following week, Agnes left.

The Abel home was a pure dovecote. They all addressed each other in sentimental aah's and little squeaks.

"He calls me pet," said the old widow. "Yes, he has names for us all."

When there were visitors, the engaged couple hung lifelessly over a couple of chairs until one of them said, "Puss puss," then they disappeared through the door.

"That's the way they talk to each other," said the widow. "Their language is a little difficult for strangers to comprehend."

When it was time for the visitors to go, there would be calls for "Pussy" and "Ducky" for a whole quarter of an hour "They must be in the garden," said the widow. Pussy and Ducky were always in the garden, hiding anywhere where there was a bit of dense greenery.

When Pussy and Ducky emerged, they looked flushed and confused.

Louise and the little man spent their time in a series of minor skirmishes and wrestling bouts. The little man gave her brother-in-law's kisses and tickled her behind the doors.

When they were in company, they were all sleepy and sat in the corners. At table, the widow used the term of endearment *liebling* for all three of "her children". She did not herself know what it meant.

If they were home during the evening, no candles were lit.

"We enjoy sitting in the gloom," said the widowed mother, "all of us."

The little man would sit on the sofa between the younger daughter Ida and the elder daughter Louise. Miss Jensen and the widow would occasionally say something in the semi-darkness. There were sounds of creaking from over on the sofa. Thus they would sit for hours on end.

When Miss Jensen arrived home she kissed Bel-Ami on its

cold nose.

Pussy and Ducky would sometimes go down across the fields to meet the evening train. They would walk up and down the platform, looking into each other's eyes; when they turned, the little man would look deep into Pussy's eyes.

Katinka sat on the platform bench wrapped in Huus' shawl; when the train had left she could hear the couple billing and cooing on their way home along the path across the meadow.

Katinka rose and went indoors. The days were drawing in, and they already needed to have some light when they had tea.

"The lamp, Marie," she said.

Marie came in and stood with the lamp over by the piano. The light fell on Katinka's diminutive, narrow face and the transparent white hands which remained there on the keys after she had played the last notes.

"Call Bai and tell him tea is ready," said Katinka. She supported herself on the piano in order to rise from the stool. She was always so tired and felt as though she had lead in her legs.

They had their tea, and Bai read the papers while drinking his toddy.

Katinka took a book from the bag. They were always the most recent books: Agnes and Andersen had always fought for them.

The book lay open beneath the lamp. Katinka never got further than twenty pages into them: this was not real life after all, and neither was it really poetry such as could keep her thoughts at bay.

She took her album out, she had written "Marianna" in it and dated it. And when she put the book back once more she stood for a while in front of the drawer before closing it again. The little Japanese tray lay there, packed in her yellowing bridal veil.

She went out into the kitchen. She had her favourite seat at the chopping block in the corner. Marie was sewing in front of the tallow candle that stood on the table, talking ceaselessly. She was a faithful soul who never forgot old affections.

She kept on talking about Huus and how lonely it had become now.

Katinka sat silently in her corner. Occasionally she would shiver as though she was cold, and she held her arms tight across her breast.

Marie continued to talk with her big red face turned towards the lone candle.

"I suppose we'd better be getting to bed," said Bai, opening the door.

"Yes, Bai."

"Good night, Marie."

Autumn arrived with its melancholy veil of mist across the meadows. The sky lay heavy above days that surreptitiously moved in semi-darkness from one night to the next.

"You must pull yourself together, you know," said the young doctor. "You must get a grip on yourself."

"Yes, doctor."

"And you must walk. You must have some exercise. There's no strength left in you at all."

"Yes, doctor. I will go for a few walks."

"Nothing new otherwise?" The doctor rose. "Have you heard from Miss Agnes?"

"Yes, I heard the other day."

"They say Andersen is applying for a job elsewhere."

"I did hear that," said Katinka. "Everyone is leaving."

"Oh no, my dear, some people are staying."

"Yes, we are staying, doctor."

"Your wife is not well," said the doctor out in the office, lighting a cigar.

"No, it's all a bit of a pickle," said Bai.

"She seems not to have any strength. Ah well, good morning, stationmaster."

"You must take a walk, Tik," said Bai as he came in after the goods train had left. "You're not doing anything to help yourself."

Katinka took a walk. She dragged herself across the meadows, fighting her way against the wind and the rain.

She went down to the chapel-at-ease. Out of breath, she rested on the ancient meeting stone outside the church. The cemetery lay there, flat and flowerless behind the white wall. Only the privet hedges stood straight around the rigid crosses bearing their inscriptions.

She went home again across the meadows. The midday train came rumbling across the bridge and snaked its way out again. The smoke from it hung there for a time like a darker patch in the grey mist and then dispersed.

They were ploughing on the other side of the river. The turf was being peeled up in long lines behind the slow-moving plough.

Katinka came home.

The miller had been there, or the bailiff from Kiær's.

"Nice chap, that man Svendsen," said Bai to Katinka. "He's got his head screwed on the right way."

"But there's no knowing what he's like at his work," he said to Kiær,

Kiær mumbled something or other.

"But he's a good chap, one of the right sort, old man."

Svendsen collected Greek cards and pictures in sealed envelopes. He brought them with him down to the station and he and Bai went through them over their toddies. "We'll just check the archives," said Svendsen.

"Aye, I don't mind that." Bai was always willing.

Svendsen had the "latest" sent from Hamburg, C.O.D.

"Filthy stuff," said Bai happily. He always spoke in a quieter voice when they were "at the archives", although the door was closed.

"Filthy stuff, Svendsen my lad," he said, holding the cards up to the lamp.

They continued to look at the cards. Bai rubbed his knees.

"But this one's tall," he said. "And this one looks difficult."

Svendsen rubbed his nose.

"That's a nice bit of meat," he said. "That's meat for you."

They had gone through all the pictures and sat quietly over their toddy glasses. It was as though Bai was drooping a little.

"Aye," he said, "but what about life, Svendsen? What's life got to offer, old man, when you have a sickly wife?"

Bai sighed and stretched out his legs.

"Aye, old man," he said. "That's how it is."

Svendsen had kept a philosophical silence. Now he rose:

"No, we haven't got a damned idea of what songs were sung at our cradle," he said.

Bai rose and opened the door to the sitting room.

"What on earth?" he said. "Are you sitting in the dark?"

"Yes." Katinka rose from her corner. "I was just sitting in the dark for a few minutes. Do you want anything, Bai?"

"I'm going to go a little way with Svendsen," said Bai.

Katinka came in to say goodbye.

"Your wife's still a bit pale around the gills," said Svendsen, feeling his pockets to make sure he had his collection with him.

"Good heavens, ma-am, you'd better stay inside. It's far too cold."

"I'm only going as far as the gate," she said.

They went onto the platform. "A lovely starry night," said Bai.

"That suggests it's going to be cold. Good night, Mrs Bai."

The gate closed.

"Good night."

Katinka stood there leaning against the gate. The voices died away.

Katinka raised her eyes. Yes, the sky was clear and all the stars were out.

As though she wanted to pour out her heart to the dead tree, Katinka bent down and threw her arms round the damp trunk.

The Lindes often came of an evening. The two old folk were missing Agnes.

And Andersen was leaving as well.

"He wanted to leave," said the old parson. "And now we risk being saddled with one of those evangelicals."

Mr Andersen had found a parish on the west coast.

Mrs Linde sat in the corner, weeping.

"Oh, heavens above, I could see it all coming," she said. "I saw it perfectly well. But they can't make their minds up, Mrs Bai. They can't make their minds up, my dear."

"That's young people today, completely different from what it was like in our day, my dear Mrs Bai. They go around wondering whether they are in love until they break off with each other and go their own way and are unhappy for the rest of their lives."

"I had my fortune told, my dear, before Linde proposed to

me, and we have taken the good with the bad for thirty years."

"But now we might be leaving Agnes behind as a lonely old maid one day when we two old ones close our eyes."

The gentlemen came in. The old minister was to have his game of whist.

Katinka was happiest when the old minister was there. It was as though he brought such a sense of peace with him.

When he sat there with a small glass, wearing his skullcap, playing a shrewd game and with a happy look on his old face.

"There we are, my dear," he said as he took the tricks.

The two old folks would argue a little.

"It's as I say, Linde."

"Well, just look, dear." And he would spread his tricks out on the table.

"It's you, Mrs Bai, it's you."

Katinka's thoughts drifted away. She sat there watching the two old people.

"Queen of diamonds. There you see, dear."

They played the last rubber with a dummy hand. Katinka went around preparing the table. They dined increasingly well at the Bais. Bai had so many favourite dishes and Katinka prepared them for him.

There were many days she spent in the kitchen from early in the morning, boiling and frying from recipes and cookery books. Difficult complicated dishes requiring both scraping and peeling.

Quite worn out, Katinka sat down on the chopping block and coughed.

"You'll be getting consumption the way you put yourself out to make sure they've got plenty to stuff themselves with," said Marie.

"Would you like a glass of gin?" says Katinka.

"If you've got some."

When he nodded, it could be seen that Bai had acquired a double chin. In general, he was putting on weight. With a coquettish little swelling beneath his waistcoat and dimples on his knuckles.

"It's ready now," says Katinka.

"Thank you, dear," says Bai.

Bai had recently taken on something of the quality of a sultan. Perhaps it was a result of his corpulence.

"Thank you, dear, we'll just finish the game," he repeats.

Katinka sits down on a chair near the table and waits. The old minister looks from Bai across the well-laid table to his quiet wife. Katinka is resting her head on her hand.

"It's you, sir," says old Linde to Bai.

Katinka rises. She has forgotten something for the table. The door closes behind her and the old minister looks again across the illuminated table at Bai, who is holding the cards over his coquettish bulge:

"Yes, inspector," says the old parson to Bai, "you are a fortunate man."

Afterwards, they sit over their milk punch and cakes. "It's the good husbands who like sweet things," says Mrs Linde. Bai helps himself to more vanilla biscuits out of the box.

And they chew away as they sit there around the lamp.

"Won't you play something for us?" says Mrs Linde.

"Or sing something, one of Agnes' songs?" says the old minister.

Katinka goes over to the piano. And in her weak voice she quietly sings the song about Marianna.

The old minister listens with his hands folded and Mrs Linde lowers her knitting.

"Deep down below the grass asleep
Lies poor, dear Marianna
Come now, oh girls, for we must weep
For poor, dear Marianna."

"Thank you," said the old minister.

"Thank you, Mrs Bai," said Mrs Linde.

She could not really see the stitches until she had dried her eyes.

Katinka remained seated there with her back to the others. The tears slowly fell from her cheeks down onto the keys.

"Aye, young people nowadays have a lot of ideas," said the old minister. He was staring vacantly in the air and thinking of Agnes.

They rose and prepared to leave, and Mrs Linde fetched her coat from the bedroom. The two candles by the looking glass were lit. It was so light and cosy in there with all the white bedclothes and the looking glass on the dressing table.

"Aye," said Mrs Linde, "if only we could see Agnes in a home like this." She was still sniffing while she tied her hatband.

"I'll go a little way with the minister," said Bai. "It's important to have a little exercise."

"Yes," said the minister. "One needs a little exercise after all that jellied eel. You eat too well here at the station. Mother here has forbidden me to set foot here on a Saturday."

"I won't come any further," said Katinka, standing at the door. "The doctor wants me to take care of my cough."

"No, go inside. Autumn is the worst time."

"Good night. Good night."

Katinka went inside. She took out an old letter from Agnes,

it was crumpled and had been read time after time, and she spread it out beneath the lamp:

"And then I had hoped that the first days would be the worst and that time would heal all wounds. But the first days are easy and nothing compared to now. For then it is a pain in which everything is near. But as everything is fading now, day by day, every new morning that wakens us is simply going to move us further and further away. And nothing new comes, Katinka, not even a shadow, but simply all the old things, memories that we rake up over and over again and ponder over... And then it is as though there were some great beast sucking the blood out of our hearts. Memories are a disaster for both body and soul."

Katinka leaned back with her head against the cold wall. Her face was pale in the light from the lamp. She had no more tears.

Bai came home.

"It got rather late," he said. "Time really does pass damned quickly... I came across Kiær somewhere or other on the way. It was Kiær who wanted to have a drink... I met him... on the way home."

"Has it really got so late?" was all that Katinka said.

"Yes, it's past one o'clock." Bai started to undress. "That's what comes of walking people home, damn it," he said.

Bai had recently always walked people "home". He went as far as the inn: "Well, I'd better be getting home to keep an eye on things," he said as he took leave of his guests.

He kept his eye on things in the inn in the company of a girl who during the summer had had short puff sleeves over a pair of soft arms. One o'clock came and then two o'clock as he "kept an eye on things."

"But you could have gone to bed, you know," he said to Katinka. "All you do is sit up and get cold."

"I didn't know it was so late."

The bed creaked under Bai as he stretched himself.

Katinka put the flowers in a row down on the floor. She coughed as she bent down.

"Blast this rheumatism," said Bai. "It hurts like hell."

"I could rub your arm for you," said Katinka.

It had become a regular evening ritual that Katinka rubbed Bai's arms with some miracle cure for rheumatism.

"Oh, never mind," said Bai. He turned over a couple of times and fell asleep.

Katinka heard the night train. It rumbled across the bridge and clattered into the station – and now it was gone.

Katinka hid her face in the sheets so as not to waken Bai with her coughing.

Winter came, and Christmas arrived. Agnes was at home and the "post office official" came to the Abels on Christmas Eve.

Little Miss Jensen and Bel-Ami were at the station just as they were last year. Bel-Ami was now being carried quite officially.

"He's gone blind," said Little Miss Jensen. The animal was so lazy that it could simply not be bothered to open its eyes.

When the tree was lit, Bai brought a sealed telegram and placed it on Katinka's table.

The telegram was from Huus.

Bai and Wee Bentzen sat dozing in the office. Katinka and Jensen sat in the sitting room, where the candles on the tree burned down.

Little Miss Jensen nodded as she dozed and bumped her

head on the piano.

Katinka looked at the tree with the dead candles. Her hand gently stroked Huus' telegram, which lay on her lap.

VI

Winter passed, and then spring and summer too, smiling and warming the meadows.

"It's a miserable state of affairs, old man," said Bai to Kiær. "I moved up into the attic yesterday. A man must have his night's sleep when he's got to see to his business during the day."

Katinka's coughing could be heard throughout the house.

Marie brought her wine and water and stood waiting by her bed. It was as though the coughing would tear Katinka apart.

"Thank you, thank you," she said. "Go back to your room now and get some sleep." She was breathing heavily.

"What time is it?"

"Half past three."

"Oh." Katinka sank back in her bed. "Is that all?"

Marie tiptoed off on bare feet to her couch, and it was not long before the sound of her deep breathing could be heard. The bright spot from the night light behind the bed could be seen projected on the motionless ceiling. Katinka closed her eyes and lay back on the pillow.

She was late up in the morning. She sat wrapped in blankets out on the platform bench in the sunshine.

The slender guard in the tight, revealing trousers was on the midday train. He jumped down and asked how she was.

"You'll see," he said, "the fresh autumn air…"

"Perhaps," said Katinka, reaching out a damp, lifeless hand to him.

Bai and the guard walked along the platform together.

"Both lungs," said Bai. He had developed a habit of wiping his eyes with his fingers.

"God's will," he said and sighed.

The train started to move. The guard jumped on board. He continued to look back at Katinka as she sat there so tiny and pale in the sunshine.

He really felt damn sorry for her, really sorry.

Aye, it was a damn shame.

There had actually been a time last winter when he had had all kinds of thoughts. She would often be sitting out there on the platform bench looking all "wistful".

He had drunk the odd toddy at Bai's on some evenings, but Bai had been going downhill.

It had just been the start of her illness.

The train trundled off on its way across the meadows. Sky and landscape were radiant in the bright autumn air.

The starlings were gathering in flocks and making a din all along the telegraph wires.

"Now they are going to leave us," said Katinka. She watched the departing birds beneath the clear sky.

The doctor came and sat with her. "Well, how do you feel?"

"I'm sitting here gathering strength," she said, "for tomorrow."

"For tomorrow? Oh, of course, it's his birthday."

"Yes."

"But you will remember your promise, Mrs Bai?"

"Yes. I'll go to bed as soon as they have had their meal."

It was Bai's birthday. Katinka wanted him to have his *Hombre* party. She had been talking about it for a long time.

She would stay up for the meal, after which they would all be going into Bai's room to play *Hombre*, and then they would simply not notice that she was ill.

"On that day, at least," she said.

"You should go indoors now," said the doctor.

"Yes." Katinka rose.

"Let me help you."

"Thank you. It's the stairs," she said. "The stairs are always a problem."

Her poor heavy feet could not manage the three small steps.

"Thank you, doctor. But could I have my shawl, please."

The doctor takes the blue shawl from the bench. "Your favourite garment," he says.

Katinka turns round in the doorway and looks out across the meadows. "It's so lovely here at this time of the year," she says.

During the afternoon, she had everything for the salads placed on the table in the sitting room. She cut up beetroot and potatoes into small pieces on a small chopping board.

Miss Jensen came in to visit. Katinka nodded.

"Yes, I can still manage this," she said. "Is there anything new?"

She leaned back. Her hands were so tired and it hurt her breast to keep her arms raised.

"I haven't seen the Abels for some time."

"They are hoping now that Barner will get a job," said Miss Jensen.

"Yes, he's trying, of course."

Little Miss Jensen is given a cup of coffee.

"Would you pass me the oil, Marie," says Katinka.

She is handed a battery of bottles and large dishes. "Oh, they are so heavy," she says. She can scarcely lift the big vinegar bottle. She tastes and stirs the bowls.

"No," she says suddenly, pushing them away.

"No, I can't taste anything any longer."

She sits there, tired and with her eyes closed. Blotches of red have spread across her face.

"But I could help you," says little Miss Jensen.

"Oh, Marie can do it. I must simply get to bed."

But throughout that afternoon Marie must bring everything for her to see as she lies there. She sits up in bed, but she has a searing pain in her chest. "Yes," she says, "Bai is used to having it like this."

Marie has to take the best china and glasses, and the fine sets of knives and forks into the bedroom and polish and rub them and set them out on the table.

Katinka lies there, counting and reckoning, her eyes burning with fever.

"I wonder whether it's all there," she says.

She lies there, a little feeble, and rubs her dry, hot face down on the pillow.

"The toddy spoons, Marie," she says then. "We've forgotten the toddy spoons."

"I suppose we can put them on Huus' tray," says Marie. She comes in with the spoons on the little Japanese tray.

"No, not on that." Katinka half rises in bed.

"Give it to me," she says. She takes the tray and holds the burning palms of her hands over the cool lacquer. She remains there, lying silently with Huus' tray in her hands.

Bai comes in and looks at all the china and glasses, which have now all been polished, made to sparkle and arranged on the table.

"This is ridiculous, my dear," he says. "Simply ridiculous. I've told you, you know. You just lie there and get worse, Tik."

He takes her hand: "Aye, you are dreadfully hot."

"Oh, it's nothing," says Katinka, gently freeing her hand from his.

"As long as there is nothing missing."

Bai starts to count.

"I suppose we're going to have some stewed fruit," he says.

"Yes."

"Oh, good. But there are no fruit plates."

"Then they have been forgotten. Yes, that's what happens when I can't be there myself to keep a check, Bai," says Katinka, sinking back into her pillows.

The company was what Bai called 'the old soap cellar'.

"You can be yourself in the soap cellar," he said. "People of like mind."

The people of like mind were three landowners, headed by Kiær, with Bai as the fourth member.

Svendsen joined them as an extra.

"He livens things up," said Bai to Katinka. Katinka had never heard Svendsen being lively. When she was present he was content to manicure his nails or to tug at his moustache.

"Just bring him along, Kiær," said Bai. "He makes up the fifth member and sits there lounging nice and quiet."

Katinka opened the door to the office herself. "It's all ready, Bai," she said.

The gentlemen came in; Katinka was fully dressed, with a tall ruff round her neck right up to her thin little face.

She sat next to Kiær at table.

They talked about her illness. Oh, they would see, winter was the best time of the year. The quiet, clear cold air gave one strength.

Yes, the quiet, clear cold air.

"Let's drink to that," said Bai. They drank. "Down the hatch," said Bai.

The men of like mind ate with their napkins pinned round their necks. They sniffed at every single mayonnaise-covered mouthful before savouring it.

"Oil," said Mortensen.

Katinka sat with some small pieces on her plate. She sat quite upright because of the pains in her chest. Her fork shook in her hand as she tried to eat. "Take it away, Marie," she said.

The ducks came in and Kiær drank to Bai. They knew his heart was in the right place and he was a good fourth hand. They drank to Kiær.

They became livelier and drank deep, toasting each other. They talked about the latest machinery and cattle prices.

"Here's to a good year, old boy."

Bai drank again.

Katinka's cheeks were burning and she saw the faces as though through a grey veil. She pressed herself firmly against the chair back and looked at Bai, who went on eating.

"It's so tender. It just lies on your tongue," Kiær declared, pouring her a glass of old burgundy.

"Thank you, thank you."

Mortensen wanted to take the liberty of making a speech. He rose and loosened the napkin from around his neck. He wanted simply to make a brief speech.

When Mortensen made a speech he became all religious. On reaching his fifth sentence he spoke unfailingly of "those who had gone before" and were looking down on them from their place in heaven.

There was always something looking down on Mortensen from his heaven.

Those of like mind sat drooping and looking down on their plates.

Katinka scarcely heard anything. She was managing to sit straight by holding onto the seat of her chair, and she turned alternately pale then flushed.

By the time he had finished, Mortensen was able to enjoy a fresh piece of duck.

"Oh, these ducks, madam! Now this is what I call roasting."

Katinka only heard the voices indistinctly, and she supported herself using the table when she rose.

The gentlemen went into the office. Katinka fell back on her chair. Bai opened the door and came in again.

"That was really good, Tik. Splendid. And you managed fine."

Katinka sat up and smiled, "Yes," she said.

"Now I will see to the toddies."

Bai went back into the office. Katinka remained at the deserted table with the bottles and the half-empty glasses.

In the office they were laughing and talking all at the same time in loud voices, Kiær louder than the rest.

"Take the lamps in," said Katinka. The peals of raucous laughter reached her each time Marie opened the door.

"You ought to be in bed, Mrs Bai," said Marie.

"I'm all right."

"All for the sake of those greedy-guts." Marie slammed the kitchen door, making Katinka start.

All that was left was a lone candle in the middle of the dining table. The big, disorderly table was a dismal sight in the gloom.

Katinka was so tired, she had to sit there in a corner for a time while she gathered her strength.

Marie went from the kitchen to the office, banging the doors.

They were certainly making merry in there. It must be Svendsen singing.

Katinka listened to the voices from her corner and watched Marie as she went through the lit-up doors with glasses and bottles.

That was how it would be one day when she was gone and forgotten.

"Marie," she said.

She attempted to get up and walk, but she grabbed at the wall and could manage no more. Marie supported her into the bedroom.

"That's what you get for putting on a show," said Marie.

Katinka had a long fit of coughing while sitting on the edge of the bed.

"Shut the doors," she said.

She continued to cough: "And Bentzen must have something to eat," she said.

"Oh, he'll get something soon enough," said Marie. She managed to undress Katinka, swearing the while.

Svendsen was singing again next door in his thick voice:

"Oh Charles, my love, do write to me
The way you used to do…"

And they chinked their glasses. "Silence," shouted Kiær. "Quietly, old friends."

Katinka had lain dozing for some time, and now she woke up. It was Bai.

"That's that ceremony over," he said. He spoke in a loud voice after all those toddies.

"Have they gone?" said Katinka. "What time is it?"

"Half past two, by Jove. Time gets on when you are with a crowd like that."

He sat down on the bed and launched into a lengthy account.

"Hell of a lot of stories that man Svendsen can tell. Damn fine stories as well." He told a few and slapped his thighs as he laughed.

Katinka lay there, burning with fever.

"But they're all damned lies," said Bai finally.

He was overcome with emotion as he said good night, and as he stood in the doorway he told one last story about Mortensen's dairymaid.

"Aye, aye, you need to get some sleep," he said.

"Good night."

"Good night."

Katinka was worse the following day. The doctor was now calling a couple of times a day.

"She's in a damned dreadful state," said Bai. "And she managed the birthday so well, doctor."

"Well, she is not managing so well now, Mr Bai," said the doctor.

No one was allowed in to see Katinka. She was to have complete rest.

Mrs Madsen from the inn knew all about that kind of thing. But surely it was possible to cheer her up a little so she did not just lie there rubbing her eyes in the dark.

Mrs Madsen came right up to the bed.

It was dark, and the blinds were drawn. "Who is that?" asked Katinka from the pillows.

"It's me. Mrs Madsen from the inn."

"Good morning," said Katinka, reaching out a burning hand.

"Oh, it's as bad as that, is it," said Mrs Madsen.

"Yes," said Katinka, turning her head a little on the pillow.

"I'm not very well."

"No, you could hardly say that," said Mrs Madsen angrily. She sat there and looked at Katinka's emaciated face in the dark.

"And it's all because of that do last night."

"It was probably a little too much."

"Yes, it was certainly a little too much," said Mrs Madsen still with the same anger in her voice.

She felt ever more furious as she sat there in the wretched dark in front of the poor pale face on the pillows.

"Aye, you could certainly say that," she said again. "And he had deserved all he got, as well."

And in her fury she told her everything about Bai and about the girl he was in the habit of visiting and how long it had been going on.

"But Gusta didn't get away with it scot free either."

Katinka had at first not understood any of it, for she was so weary and slow.

Then, like a flash of lightning, she understood and opened her eyes for a moment and looked straight up at Mrs Madsen.

"And some people work themselves to death for a man like that," said Mrs Madsen.

She fell silent and waited for Katinka to say something.

But Katinka lay there without moving. A couple of tears could be seen on her cheeks.

"Oh dear," said Mrs Madsen, "I'd probably not have been much wiser myself."

Mrs Madsen had left.

"Marie," said Katinka, "would you draw the curtains back so I can have a little light."

Marie drew the curtains back, allowing the daylight to fall on the bed.

"Why are you crying, ma'am?" she said.

Katinka lay turned towards the light.

"Is it your chest?" said Marie.

"No, no," said Katinka. "I'm all right."

She continued to weep, silently and happily.

Her weeping ceased, and she lay there in the same position, weary, in inexpressible peace.

The last sunny days of autumn arrived. During the bright late mornings, Katinka lay with the sun shining directly on her bed. She invented so many happy dreams as her hands gently slid to and fro over the sun-warmed coverlet.

"You look well," said Marie.

"Yes, and I feel well." She nodded without opening her eyes and lay there again silent in the sun.

"I'll get up again tomorrow," she said.

"You'll be able to."

Katinka turned over to face the window. "It's like late summer," she said. "If I could just get out tomorrow."

She continued to talk about it. If only she could get out. Down to the summerhouse by the elder bush.

Were there still leaves on the elder? And the rose? And the cherry tree?

"They were all in flower last year, a whole host of flowers."

"There were enough for the entire village to bottle them while you were away," said Marie.

"All that white blossom."

Katinka continued to talk about the garden. Time after time she said, "Do you think he will let me? Do you think I might be allowed?"

"Perhaps, when the sun is shining."

The doctor did not come, and that afternoon Marie had to

go down and ask.

It was dark before she returned. Katinka lay there without a light. She rang the small bell beside the bed.

"Has she not come?" she said.

"She had to walk all that way, you know," said Bai.

"It's taking such a long time," said Katinka. Her cheeks were flushed with fever.

She lay listening for every door that opened or closed.

"That was the kitchen door," she said.

It was a man selling brushes.

"She's not coming," said Katinka.

"You'll make yourself ill again," said Bai.

She lay there quietly, no longer ringing or speaking. Then she heard Marie open the office door and lay there with a beating heart under the coverlet and without speaking.

"What did he say?" said Bai out there.

"About half an hour in the middle of the day when the sun is out," said Marie. "Is your wife asleep?"

"I think so."

Marie tiptoed in. Katinka lay there for a moment without moving.

"Is it you?" she said.

"Yes, he said you can get up for a time and sit in the sun in the middle of the day."

Katinka did not reply immediately. Then she grasped Marie's hand:

"Thank you," she said. "You are so kind, Marie."

"Oh, how hot your hands are, Mrs Bai."

Katinka lay in a fever that night, she lay there with eyes glistening and had no sleep. But it was almost morning before she woke Marie.

Marie looked out of the sitting-room window.

"The sky looks clear," she said. "Let's see how the weather turns out."

"Look out of the kitchen door," said Katinka from her bed. "That's always where you can see the clouds coming."

The sky was clear from the kitchen door too.

"I can manage on my own. I'm all right," said Katinka. "She supported herself along the corridor walls across to the door and out to the platform.

"It's lovely and warm," she said.

"Mind the step now. There, that's right." Walking on the gravel was difficult. She put her arms up on Marie's shoulders. "My head feels so heavy," she said.

She stopped at every third step to look out across the meadows over to the woods. It was as though the sun was imparting radiance to every leaf.

Katinka wanted to go across to the platform gate. She stood leaning on it for a moment.

"It's so lovely," she said, "this little forest of ours."

Katinka looked right out along the sun-drenched road: "The milestone is over there," she said.

She turned her head and looked out across the fields and the meadows and the radiant sky.

"Yes," she said in a scarcely audible voice, "it's so lovely here."

Marie went along drying her eyes when Katinka was not looking.

"But see how the leaves are falling," said Katinka. She turned and took a couple of steps on her own.

They came out into the garden.

Katinka spoke no more. They went round the lawn down to the summerhouse.

"The elder," was all she said. "I can sit here."

Marie wrapped the rugs around her and she sat there huddled up, gazing silently across the sun-drenched garden.

The leaves from the cherry trees still lay yellow on the lawn; a couple of small roses were still in flower.

Marie made to pluck them.

"No," said Katinka, "that would be a pity – leave them."

She sat again. Her lips were moving as though she was whispering.

"This is where Huus best liked to sit," said Marie. She was standing beside the bench.

Katinka started. Then, with a quiet smile, she said, "Yes, he liked sitting here."

They started to walk again.

When they reached the gate, Katinka stood in silence for a moment. She looked back, into the garden.

"I wonder who will walk in there now?" she said.

She was so tired. She leaned heavily on Marie and in the corridor she supported herself against the walls.

"Open the back door," she said, "so that I can see the forest."

She went over and leant for a moment on the doorpost, looking out in the direction of the forest and the road.

"Marie," she said, "I would like to see the pigeons as well."

Katinka no longer got up. Her strength was deserting her more and more.

Mrs Abel brought her wine jelly.

"It will make your tongue feel fresher," she said. She sat looking at Katinka through eyes blinded by tears.

"And you are so alone lying there."

Mrs Abel would send her elder daughter Louise.

"She is as good as a trained nurse," she said, "my elder

daughter, as good as a trained nurse."

Louise came in the mornings and tiptoed around in a white pinafore. Katinka lay there as though asleep. Louise laid the table for lunch and made the coffee.

And the door to the bedroom was left ajar while they had their meal.

Bai was very grateful. The widow dried her eyes. "You know your friends when you are in need," she said.

Mrs Linde came in the afternoon and sat knitting by the bed. She had lots of things to tell about the entire neighbourhood, some new, some old. And also about herself and her husband.

Old Linde came to fetch his wife at dusk, and the two old folk sat by the bed in the twilight for another hour.

Agnes was their sole subject of conversation.

"Linde can't live without Agnes," said Mrs Linde. She herself wept secretly both morning and evening.

"Aye, my dear, it has to be admitted that she's the apple of my eye," said the old minister.

"You'll see, she'll come home one day," said Katinka.

"As an old maid." Mrs Linde's knitting needles clicked away.

Mrs Linde could not forget those words about an "old maid".

They sat chatting, and the old minister had a blackcurrant toddy before going home.

"It does one good," he said, "and it doesn't go to your head."

The two old folk trundled home along a road that was dark in the autumn dusk.

Bai was out quite frequently.

"A little game of *Hombre* to buck you up," said Kiær. "It'll do you good, old man."

"Yes, old friend." Bai wiped his hands across his eyes.

"Some time later in the week," he said. "Thank you."

"Thank you for being such a good friend." He clapped Kiær on the shoulder and was quite emotional. Bai had become quite emotional recently.

He went out and played *Hombre* into the small hours.

When he arrived home, he woke Katinka because he 'couldn't go to bed without seeing how she was'.

"Thank you," said Katinka. "Have you had a good time?"

"As good a time as I can have," said Bai, "with you lying here." He sat sighing by the bed for some time, until he had Katinka wide awake.

"Good night," he said then.

"Sleep well, Bai."

When Marie was outside during the day, the doors were left open into the office. Katinka lay listening for the tapping of the telegraph.

"It's so busy," she said. "So much to say."

"Bai," she shouted. "There's one for here."

Bai swore roundly out in the office.

"Yes, by Jove there is." He appeared in the doorway. "It's for the parsonage."

"The parsonage." Katinka raised herself up in bed. "It must be from Agnes."

Bai said nothing, he was all excited, he ran about with his blue pencil looking for his jacket and he wrote the telegram down, in his shirt sleeves, and got it wrong and tore it up.

"Bai," said Katinka, "Bai, is it Agnes?"

"Yes, by Gad."

Bai rushed off personally with the telegram just as the afternoon train was due.

He had never seen such joy before. The two old folk both laughed and cried.

"Oh, thank God. Just fancy that it really is true. Oh dear, is it really true?"

"Yes, my dear. Yes, it really is." The old parson tried to remain composed.

He patted her head in an effort to calm her down.

But then he folded his hands. "No," he said, "it's too much."

And he wept and dried his eyes on his velvet skullcap.

"Oh dear," he said, "praised be the Lord, I say. God be praised."

The old minister wanted to give Katinka the news himself, and he got his coat, his hat and his gloves, and he put them all down again and took hold of Bai with both hands:

"Oh, how wonderful, stationmaster," he said, "for us two old folk here to have this experience, to experience this, stationmaster."

"Aye, we all have our way."

"Andersen had to learn to miss her, yes, to miss her," said the old minister.

He pottered about but failed to get ready.

His wife came in with strawberry liqueur before they left.

The old minister whistled an old soldiers' song as he walked along.

He sat by Katinka's bed.

"Aye," he said, "God brings the right people together."

Agnes came home about a week later.

She stormed across the platform and rushed in through the office. From the doorway leading into the house she saw Katinka lying there on the pillow with her eyes closed. Agnes would not have recognised her.

Katinka opened her eyes and looked at her:

"Yes," she said, "it's me."

Agnes went across and took Katinka's hands. She knelt down by her bed.

"Lovely lady," said Agnes, fighting to prevent herself from weeping.

She came every afternoon and sat with Katinka until the evening.

They did not speak much. Katinka dozed and Agnes lowered her sewing onto her lap and looked at the poor face on the pillow. Katinka was breathing weakly, and each breath rattled in her breast.

Katinka moved, and Agnes took hold of her sewing again and worked the needle out and in.

Katinka lay there, awake. She was so weak that she was unable to speak. The coughing came and shook her, she rose up in the bed, it was as though she was being torn apart.

Agnes supported her. Katinka was drenched in cold sweat. "Thank you," she said. "Thank you."

She settled again and lay silent. From inside the bed curtain she looked at Agnes' face, so round and strong, and at her hands as they moved resolutely over her sewing.

"Agnes," she said "will you play something for me?"

"You should get some sleep," said Agnes.

"Oh no. Play something."

Agnes rose and went over to the piano. She quietly played melody after melody.

Katinka lay still with her hands on the blanket.

"Agnes," she said, "Won't you sing that song for me?"

It was the song about Sorrento. Agnes sang it in her deep contralto voice:

> "There the tall and darkling pines
> Give their shade to ambrosial vines

There orange grove and luscious lime
Their perfumes give to this sweet clime;
There boats rock gently by the shore
As happy lovers by the score
Loudly the Madonna's praises sing
And then to her their prayers do bring."

She stayed by the piano for a time. Then she rose and went into the bedroom.

"Thank you," said Katinka.

She lay there for a moment.

"Yes," she said softly. "How lovely life could be."

Agnes stretched out by the bed. The two of them lay there in silence in the dark, Katinka's hand stroking Agnes' hair.

"Agnes," she said. "I don't want a funeral oration."

"But Katinka."

"Just a prayer," she said.

She was silent again. Agnes wept quietly. Katinka continued to twist tiny locks of her hair round her fingers.

"But there is just," she spoke quite quietly and almost hesitantly, and her hand fell from Agnes' hair, "one hymn that I would very much like to have sung over my grave."

She whispered in a voice that was scarcely audible. Agnes lay there with her head buried in the pillow.

"The wedding hymn," said Katinka quite quietly, like a child scarcely daring to ask for something.

Agnes was racked with weeping and she took Katinka's hands and kissed them as she sobbed.

"But Katinka, my dear Katinka."

Katinka put her hands round her head and leant forward a little.

"Now you two are going to be so happy," she said.

She lay there silently. Agnes continued to weep.

The following day, Katinka was given the last rites by the old minister. Bai was in town.

Agnes was awakened during the night by a frightened maid holding a tallow candle. "There's a message, miss, from the station. You must come straight away."

"A message?" Agnes was up immediately.

"Who is it?" she said.

She shouted down through the corridor.

"It's me," said Wee Bentzen.

Agnes came out, wrapped in shawls.

"She's dying, miss," said Wee Bentzen. He stood there pale and with teeth chattering. Wee Bentzen had never seen anyone die before.

"Have you sent for the doctor?" said Agnes. "Give me the lamp, Ane."

"There was no one to send."

Agnes lit the lamp and went across the courtyard. She knocked on the door to the farm hands' room. It echoed in the barn.

"Lars, Lars."

The horses grew restless in their stalls.

Lars emerged at the half door in the light from the lamp, heavy with sleep.

Agnes went back across the courtyard to the front door. Wee Bentzen had gone out onto the steps, afraid of standing there in the dark.

"You come with me," said Agnes and went past them.

A couple of frightened maids came out into the corridor. "Make some coffee," said Agnes. "Be quick."

She went in to dress. Wee Bentzen was left alone in the

corridor. The doors were open throughout the house, creaking in the dark. The maids were rummaging around, half dressed and sleepy, each holding a tallow candle. They forgot a candle stick on the table. The light was flickering in the draught.

Out in the courtyard, the lad came along with the stable lantern. He put it down on the stones and went again. A ring of light was created around the lamp in the darkness.

The coach-house door was opened, and they emerged with the horses. Every sound was loud and frightening in the night.

Agnes came out and passed Bentzen in the corridor.

"I'll go down," she said. "Is she having convulsions?"

"She was crying out," said Bentzen.

Agnes looked out into the yard. "Hurry," she shouted. The boy ran across the yard with the lamp.

A couple of flickering candles were put in the kitchen window so that the light fell on the horses and carriage,

Old Mrs Linde appeared in the dining room, wearing a dressing gown belonging to the old minister. "Go back to bed, mother," said Agnes.

"Oh, Lord help us, Lord help us," said old Mrs Linde. "So it's come all of a sudden, all of a sudden." And she started wandering around with a candle in her hand like all the others.

The boy opened the gates. The noise made them all start. And Lars emerged in the kitchen door and was given a cup of coffee.

Wee Bentzen came out and sat up on the box. He saw Mrs Linde's face: she was weeping gently in the sitting room and rocking to and fro in front of the flickering candle.

They set out through the gate, down the road, through the darkness, trotting so that the willow hedge flew past them like dancing ghosts.

Lars held tight onto the reins.

"The animals are nervous when they're going to a death," he said.

They said no more. The willows were restless as the lights from the carriage flew past them.

Bai was walking up and down in the hall, up and down along the wall.

"Is it you, is it you?" he said. "Oh, she is shouting so."

Agnes opened the door to the office. She could hear Katinka groaning and the night nurse's voice saying, "There, there, there."

Marie appeared, "The doctor," she said.

"He's gone for him," said Agnes.

She went in. The night nurse was holding Katinka's arms above her head. The spasms were convulsing her body beneath the blankets.

"Hold on to her," said the nurse.

Agnes took hold of her wrists and released them again when she felt the cold sweat.

The dying woman was flailing around in the bed curtain with arms twisted in convulsions.

"Keep hold of her," said the nurse. Agnes took hold of her arms. "Her tongue, her tongue," she said. "Get a spoon then, her tongue."

Katinka sank back. Bluish white foam appeared over her lips, which were opened over her clenched teeth.

Marie dropped the spoon and could not find it on the floor and rummaged around with the candle searching for another.

"Keep hold of her head," said the nurse. "Keep hold of her head." Marie held it, trembling all over.

"Oh, heavens above, oh Jesus," she repeated. "Oh Jesus, dear Saviour."

Agnes pressed Katinka's arms down. "Keep her head back," said the nurse. She stretched across and pressed the spoon down between the dying woman's teeth.

Foam came and covered the spoon, "Good," whispered the nurse, "good."

Katinka opened her eyes. She fixed them on Agnes, huge and afraid.

Katinka continued to stare at her with the same look.

"Katinka."

The dying woman groaned and sank back. The spoon fell from her mouth.

"She's quietening down," said the nurse.

Katinka's eyes closed. Agnes let go of her arms.

They sat down each on her own side of the bed, listening to her breathing, which was irregular and quite weak.

"She's settling," said the nurse.

The dying woman dozed, groaning now and again.

A carriage was heard outside on the road. The door was flung open and the doctor's voice was heard.

Agnes rose and hushed him.

"She's asleep," she said.

The doctor went in and bent over the bed. "Yes," he said, "It won't be long now."

"Is she suffering?" asked Agnes.

"There's no knowing," said the doctor.

"She's asleep now."

The doctor and Agnes sat down in the sitting room. They could hear Bai walking up and down in the office.

Agnes rose and went to him.

"What does he say?" asked Bai, continuing to walk up and down.

Agnes made no reply. She sat silently on her chair.

"I never thought it would come to this," said Bai. "I never imagined this, Miss Agnes."

He wandered up and down, from door to window, stopped again by Agnes' chair and, without looking at her, said, "I never imagined it, Miss Agnes."

The doctor opened the door. "Come in here," he said.

The convulsions had started again. Bai was to hold one of her arms.

But he let go of it again.

"I can't," he said and went off with his hands to his face. They heard him sobbing in the office.

"Wipe her forehead," said the doctor.

Agnes wiped the sweat from her forehead.

"Thank you," said Katinka, opening her eyes. "Is it Agnes?"

"Yes, Katinka, it's Agnes."

"Thank you."

Then she went off again.

Towards morning, she woke. They were all sitting by her bed.

Her eyes were glazed.

"Bai," she said.

"Yes."

"Ask her to play for me."

"Do play something," said the doctor.

Agnes went into the sitting room. Her tears ran down on to the keys and onto her hands as she played without hearing what she was playing.

Katinka lay there in silence. There was a rattling in her chest as she breathed.

"Why isn't she playing?" she said.

"But she is playing, Tik."

"She can't hear any longer."

The dying woman shook her head, "I can't hear it," she said.

"The hymn," she whispered. "The hymn."

She lay for a time again, quite quiet. The doctor sat there, taking her pulse, and looking at her face.

Then she sat up and tore her hand free.

"Bai," she screamed. "Bai."

Agnes rose and rushed into the office. They all stood by the bed. Bai knelt, sobbing.

Then they all started. It was the telegraph that could be heard in all the rooms as it announced the arrival of the train.

Katinka opened her eyes. "Look, look," she said, raising her head.

"See, the sun," she said. "See the sun over the mountains."

She raised her arms; they sank again and slipped down the bedspread.

The doctor quickly bent down over the bed.

Agnes knelt at the foot with her head against the bed alongside Marie.

All that was to be heard was loud sobbing.

The doctor raised the hanging arms and folded her hands over the dead woman's breast.

"Hmm, you don't look as though you've had much sleep, Bentzen."

The guard leapt from the train.

"How is she doing?"

"She's dead," said Wee Bentzen. He spoke as though he was cold.

"What? Good God!"

The guard stood for a moment looking at the little station building, everything seemed to be as usual.

Then he turned round and quietly climbed the steps.
The train was hidden by the winter mists over the meadows.

VII

It was the first day of winter. The air was clear and a thin layer of snow lay on the slightly frozen ground.

Outside the church, the men were beginning to congregate, solemn, wearing silk top hats of many vintages. They stood whispering in small groups, and one by one they went and looked down in the empty grave by the wall.

Inside the church, four or five were moving silently around the coffin, quietly feeling the wreaths. The parish clerk and little Miss Jensen were putting the hymn numbers up.

They were ready. "And hymn number 753 at the graveside," said little Miss Jensen.

Little Miss Jensen was a kind of funeral director on this occasion. She had immediately taken charge of the body both at home and in the church. The institute had been closed for the 'autumn holiday' since the death.

Miss Jensen looked around the church and approached the coffin accompanied by the parish clerk. The garlands were draped in regular arches above the choir and lengths of crape had been draped around the altar candles.

"Nice coffin, considering the time of year," said the parish clerk.

They stood looking at the wreaths.

"They make nice wreaths in the mill," said Miss Jensen

"Some are quite different though," said the parish clerk,

shrugging and looking down at a wreath from the Abels.

"Yes," said Miss Jensen, "they take very little interest there."

Miss Jensen retired a little and considered the coffin with a critical eye.

"Yes," she said. "I'm glad we decided on oak."

"It is, if I can put it that way, cleaner for the body," said the parish clerk.

The bells began to ring, and Miss Jensen went out into the churchyard. She greeted her pupils' fathers and took a head count.

Bai came in through the gate with two gentlemen wearing foot muffs; all hats were raised. Little Miss Jensen shook hands with people in the porch.

When all were seated in the pews, the Abel family arrived. The widow headed them; she looked as though she had been hurrying. The two chicks were veiled like two widows.

Louise placed a cross of ivy on the coffin.

Agnes sat beside the old minister. She did not hear the singing and did not open her hymn book. She just sat there, staring through misty eyes at the lovely lady's coffin.

The singing came to an end. The old minister rose and went forward.

When he saw him standing there before the coffin with his hands folded, Bai burst into tears and sobbed loudly.

The old minister waited silently, with his eyes trained on the coffin. He spoke in a soft voice. The wintry sun shone in through the choir windows on the coffin and the flowers.

The old minister spoke of those whose lives were quiet and lived in obscurity.

She was quiet, her life was quiet, and she would be brought quietly to her final resting place. The Lord God, who knows

His flock, had given her a life in quiet happiness with a good husband. He gave her a death in peace supported by the Holy Spirit. May He receive her spirit, He who alone knows hearts and reigns. May He, the sole comforter, give comfort to those who now mourn. Amen.

Old Linde fell silent. There was silence everywhere.

The pall bearers came forward with the parish clerk and Little Miss Jensen, who removed the wreaths from the coffin.

And everyone, standing in the pews, watched the coffin being carried out to the sound of the wedding hymn.

> "How fair it is to walk as one
> For two who fain would share their morrow
> Their blessed joy is never done
> And halved is the weight of sorrow.
> Aye, bliss it is
> For two to walk
> When linked by love."

Agnes continued to watch the coffin. The doors had been thrown open wide to the brightness of the day.

> "When linked by love…"

They came to the grave. It was heavy going for the pall bearers. The grave digger fumbled with the rope, and it dropped down into the grave.

Everyone stood and waited for them to get hold of the end of the rope and fix it round the coffin.

Bai held onto a bush as though he intended to break it in two as the coffin was pushed forward and sank into the ground.

Agnes had closed her eyes.

177

"How sad it is but then to part
For two who fain their days would share
But God be praised, in His own heart
Awaits us all a dwelling fair.
Aye, bliss it is
For two to walk
When linked by love."

"Come on now, brother-in-law." The two men wearing foot muffs were supporting a sobbing Bai.

The hymn came to an end. All was silent. There was not a sound. No wind blew over the bared heads.

The sand was heavy as it fell from old Linde's shaking hands.

"Our Father, who art in Heaven…"

It was all over. The two gentlemen in foot muffs shook people's hands and thanked them for "their profound sympathy".

Mrs Abel stopped them at the gate. She had a small table at home laid ready for Bai and his brothers-in-law.

"Just a modest little bite so that you don't have to eat on your own."

Mrs Abel dried her eyes.

"I know what it is to lose someone," she said.

The mourners had left.

Agnes stood by the grave alone. She looked down on the coffin with its wreaths all discoloured by the sand.

And she stared out across the roads where all the people were going back to their lives at home.

There was Bai between the two ladies in their mourning

veils, those long veils, and the two gentlemen with the foot muffs, Katinka's brothers, who had thanked the assembled mourners on behalf of the family.

Little Miss Jensen was to eat in the mill after all her efforts. Miss Helene complained about her boots being too small.

There they went, all of them.

Hurrying away.

Agnes bent her head. She felt a kind of angry revulsion at all this petty life hurrying off in all directions to get home.

She heard someone approaching from behind. It was Wee Bentzen, carrying a large box.

"It's a wreath, Miss," he said. "I wanted to bring it myself. It came by the midday train."

Wee Bentzen took the wreath out of the box.

"It's from Huus," he said.

"From Huus," said Agnes. She took the wreath and looked at the partly withered roses, "It must have been very beautiful."

"Aye," said Bentzen. "It must have been pretty."

They stood there for a moment. Agnes sank almost to her knees and gently lowered the wreath onto the coffin. The rose petals were scattered by the fall.

When Agnes turned round, Wee Bentzen was weeping as he stood there.

A workman approached.

"If you don't mind, ma'am, I need to close the churchyard."

"All right, we're coming."

"I'm sure the parish clerk will not object to my staying here," said Agnes.

Agnes and Bentzen walked quietly along the path. The workman was already standing by the gate, waiting for them.

With her hands in the pockets of her cape, Agnes stood there and watched the workman as he closed the gate and locked up.

Wee Bentzen was still sniffing a little as he said goodbye.
Agnes stood for a long time before the locked gate.

Bai spent a lot of time at the Abels.

Mrs Abel could not stand the idea of his being down there alone, in all those empty rooms, "when they themselves were able to sit around a cosy lamp," she said.

She and Louise called for him after the eight o'clock train had left.

"Just to sit around the lamp at home," said Mrs Abel.

Louise was quite at home at the station. She had to rush around and water the flowers before they left.

Mrs Abel stood and watched.

"They were the dear girl's favourites," she said in a gentle voice.

The dear girl was Katinka.

"What about the hanging basket?" said Louise. "That gets thirsty as well." She nodded in the direction of the hanging basket.

Bai had to hold the chair when Louise watered the hanging basket. She stood on her toes holding the watering can and revealing her beauty.

"She doesn't forget anything," said Mrs Abel. The hanging basket was watered so profusely that it splashed down onto the floor.

"I'm sure Marie will wipe it up," said Louise in a sharp voice in the direction of the kitchen. She always stood for a second or so in the doorway to the larder to "take stock". Louise had extremely quick fingers when something sweet had been left on a plate.

They went home to sit round the lamp.

Dressed in a white pinafore, Louise poured the tea.

Ida had to be called time after time.

"She is writing," said the widow, from her corner.

Ida always wrote in a curious state of undress.

"I think you've forgotten your cuffs, dearest," said the widow.

"Oh," said Ida. Dear little Ida was generally somewhat disorganised.

"*He's* simply not here," said the widow.

After tea, Bai was given his toddy while he read *The Morning Telegraph*. Louise did some embroidery. The widow sat and looked "tenderly" at them.

"You must simply feel you are at home. That's all we want."

When Bai had finished his newspaper, Louise played the piano. She finished with one of the little melodies Katinka had been fond of playing.

"Your dear wife used to play that," said the widow, looking at the portrait of Katinka surrounded by a wreath of everlasting flowers hanging beneath the mirror over the sofa.

"Aye," said Bai. He sat with his hands clasped. Up there by the lamp, after his toddy, Bai always felt some gentle emotion deriving from his "loss".

The widow understood him.

"But one has the glorified memory," she said. "And the promise of meeting again."

"Yes."

Bai wiped two fingers over his eyes.

They spoke about "his dear late wife" while Bai drank his second glass.

Little Miss Jensen sat by her window listening in the dark, to discover when he left.

Little Miss Jensen had spent most of her time at the parsonage recently.

"I don't think the Abels want to be disturbed," said Little Miss Jensen.

Miss Jensen had frequently visited the station during the first weeks after the death.

"A woman helps where she can," she said at the mill.

"Yes," said the miller's wife.

Miss Helene stretched out her legs and looked at her felt slippers.

"Oh, that dear Katinka spoiled him so dreadfully." Miss Jensen had taken to calling her Katinka since she had died.

Little Miss Jensen assumed a kind of supervisory function at the station.

"What need do you have of a maid?" she said.

She would come after school with a basket and Bel-Ami. Bel-Ami had his own basket near the stove.

She went around noiselessly making Bai's favourite dishes.

After the meal, she put on her coat. But Bai said she should stay and share the last bit of food with him.

"Yes, if you would rather I stayed," said Little Miss Jensen.

"At least it is a living person near you," she said modestly.

Bel-Ami was returned to his place, and they had their meal.

Little Miss Jensen did not force conversation on him. She sat there silent and sympathetic while Bai saw to his favourite dishes. He had started to recover his appetite.

After the meal they played an almost wordless game of piquet.

Miss Jensen left at ten o'clock.

"I will go by way of the grave," she said, "and put a flower on it."

Miss Jensen tended the grave.

She heard Bel-Ami whining as she went along the road home. She did not pick him up.

Miss Jensen walked deep in thought. She was thinking of selling her school.

She had always been more suited to a post in which an educated lady played the part of the lady of the house.

But for the past two or three months Miss Jensen had not been coming to the station very frequently.

She did not wish to be considered pushing.

She simply did not understand Mrs Abel.

She would sit at the window of an evening, listening to hear whether he was allowed to go home at all.

"I look after the grave," she said in the mill.

"Good Lord, those women are all over the place." Kiær waved his hat around in the office as though to keep the flies away. Louise had darted past him in the doorway.

"Good God, they do scuttle around," said Kiær.

Kiær was going to Copenhagen and wanted Bai to go with him.

"You need to, my lad. Damn it all, you really do need to. To get some air in your lungs. Like a young bachelor. Off to the skittle alley," he said.

Bai could not really make up his mind to go, so soon after.

But it would be good to have some fresh air in his lungs. Yes, he certainly needed that.

They left a week later. Mrs Abel and Louise packed his suitcase.

Bai stretched out in his seat and tensed the muscles in his arms as they started out.

"Out on your travels?" said the indiscreet guard. They came across him at a station.

"A trip for the squires. Two cheerful young bloods." The indiscreet guard produced a loud click of his tongue.

Bai said, "Aye, we're going to see how things are rubbing along."

He slapped both Kiær's knees and repeated, "Rubbing along, old man."

The train started to move and they waved to the guard, who shouted something after them.

They suddenly grew quite merry, breaking out in coarse language and slapping their thighs.

"Well, here we go again, we're off once more," said Bai.

"Well, what else are we here for?" said Kiær.

"Old Adam, you know," said Bai.

They laughed and talked. Kiær was happy.

"I'm beginning to recognise you again now," he said, "you old lamplighter. Now we can recognise you."

Bai suddenly became serious:

"Yes, old boy," he said. "It's been a sad time."

He sighed twice and sat back in the seat.

Then in a happy voice he said, "Tell you what – we'll get hold of Nielsen."

"Nielsen?" said Kiær.

"A young lieutenant, you know, a connoisseur. Of course, we don't know all the new places, old boy. I met him in the parsonage. A right lad he is, a connoisseur."

"Well, in for a penny."

They started to yawn and fell silent. They dozed off each on his own seat and slept until they reached Fredericia.

There they drank one cognac after another to counter the "cold night air".

Bai went out onto the platform. The coaches were being shunted and voices were drowned out by the ringing of bells and signalling.

Bai stood under a lamp in the midst of the crowd and

allowed himself to be pushed and shoved.

"I say, old man," he said to Kiær, rubbing his hands as he looked down the platform and the railway line, "What do you think of this?"

"This is the life," said Kiær.

The ladies were elegantly going up and down the steps, flushed with sleep, in their travelling bonnets.

"And what ladies," said Bai.

People were shouting and bells were ringing.

"Passengers for Strib."

"Passengers for the ferry."

The train carrying Bai to Copenhagen arrived at half past ten.

They found Lieutenant Nielsen on a fourth floor in Dannebrogsgade. His furniture consisted of a wardrobe with a half-open door revealing a lone uniform waistcoat and a cane chair plus a washbowl.

The lieutenant was stretched out on a straw mattress on the bedboards.

"Camping out," he said. "I have my respectable lodgings 'elsewhere', stationmaster."

Bai said they wanted to 'look around town'.

"We'd like to see certain 'places' like – you know," he said.

Lieutenant Nielsen knew.

"You want to see the market," he said. "Leave it to me. We'll see the market."

He put on his trousers and started to shout for a Mrs Madsen. Mrs Madsen reached in a naked arm holding a bar of soap.

"You see, I'm like one of the family," said the lieutenant, soaping his arms with Mrs Madsen's soap.

They agreed on a place to meet where they could look at the legs dancing in the Casino. "And then we'll go and have a look at the market," said Bai.

The lieutenant got ten øre out of Mrs Madsen and they set off straight away to the "local".

The local was a nice little beer garden in Pileallé, where "the lads" spent their time playing skittles or cards.

The "lads" were three second lieutenants and two flaxen-haired gentlemen from the national school of agriculture.

When Nielsen arrived, the gentlemen were already playing *Hombre*, sitting in shirt sleeves and with their hats on the backs of their heads.

"Well, twins," said Nielsen. "Everything all right?"

"Doing our best," said one of those with flaxen hair, shrugging his shoulders.

"Vaguely," said one of the lieutenants.

"Very vaguely," said the other,

The group took great pleasure in the expression "vaguely". They said it once every quarter of an hour in a curious tone and accompanied by tiny flicks of the hand.

"Vaguely."

"We need to water things down a bit," said Nielsen.

The group watered things down with beer and "the weaker sex".

"I've discovered a couple of big spenders," said Nielsen.

"Spenders... what the hell do you mean, Nielsen?" The flaxen-haired couple pushed their hats to the back of their heads.

"A couple of rather older big spenders, twins..."

The twins banged their bottles of beer on the table in his honour.

That evening, they went to the Attic after Nielsen had taken a look at the "dancing legs" together with Kiær and Bai.

Nielsen found some rosy-cheeked girls who drank some

punch with them and coquettishly rapped the fingers of "the two elderly gentlemen from the provinces".

Bai employed some long forgotten words from his days as a lieutenant.

The two with the flaxen hair could not stand anything. They lolled about and said, "Ugh, you old rakes," and draped themselves over Bai's and Kiær's shoulders.

They all went on drinking.

"Ugh, you old nonsense."

"Keep your hands off me." Bai had become sensitive as a result of all his drinking.

Bai did not know how it all happened. The lieutenants had suddenly disappeared with the rosy-cheeked girls.

"They've gone," said Kiær.

"Are you sitting there all on your own, gentlemen?"

It was a rather older little lady who came over to their table.

A week had passed.

Kiær had business to attend to in the mornings. Bai slept most of the time.

Kiær came home and entered their room.

"What, are you asleep?" he said.

"Aye, I don't feel in particularly good form," said Bai from the sofa, rubbing his eyes. "What time is it?"

"Two o'clock."

"Then we must be off," Bai rose from the sofa. "This is as hard as a confounded ironing board," he said. He was sore all over.

He got himself dressed.

They were going out to look at gravestones. Bai was going to buy Katinka's gravestone in Copenhagen.

He had been to three or four stonemasons without being able to make up his mind.

Kiær was impatient at the thought of having to go all over the place with him to look at those gravestones.

"It's nice of you, old friend. It's very nice of you. But it makes not a damn bit of difference to her."

Bai was rather affected as he went around among all these crosses and columns with their marble doves and angel heads.

He would have to make his mind up today; it was their last day.

He took a large, grey cross with a couple of marble hands clasped beneath a butterfly symbolising life.

"Lovely idea," he said, rubbing his eyes with a finger, "Faith, Hope and Charity."

Kiær did not always understand what Bai meant when he expressed his grief.

"Aye, nice idea," he said.

They went to the Royal Theatre that evening.

After the performance, they were to go out to the entertainment district.

"Not on your life, damn it," said Kiær, "I'm not going just to sit around and wait for that crowd."

Kiær went home.

Bai drifted around alone. There was damn well not going to be anyone able to say that he could not keep going to the very end.

He entered the place. None of the others had come as yet, and he sat down up in the gallery to wait.

No, thank you. He didn't want anything to drink – perhaps a soda water.

He sat there and through the tobacco smoke looked down into the main hall first at the eight girls sitting in a circle on the stage and then at the audience:

"Bloody kids, that's all."

"Disappointing lot," he thought. He sat there, looking down, with his cheek in his hand.

"Kids," he said again.

Then they started shouting and banging their walking sticks down there. It was for an English dancer energetically throwing her skirts up over her head. Bai had seen those same skirts flying there each evening.

And he looked almost angrily down on the enthusiasm of those banging their walking sticks.

"As if that was worth getting enthusiastic about," he said.

He swallowed his soda water and continued to look down at the main hall. The eight girls sitting there like a row of sleepy hens on a perch, and the boys laughing their heads off in order to persuade themselves it was amusing.

He had been waiting for almost three quarters of an hour, and the bunch had failed to arrive.

In any case, he was quite happy to see them stay away with their "rosy-cheeked lasses".

He could surely find some old girl for himself.

These two "old rakes from the provinces" with hair like pigs' bristles.

Bai looked over at the other side: a couple of young gentlemen were fooling around with two girls. One of them was young and lively, with a couple of little dimples.

The young man bent forward and stole some kisses beneath her veil.

The others had still not arrived. And Bai felt something like irritation, like anger, while all the time watching this pair of doves billing and cooing.

No one was coming, damn it.

Oh well, when they've fleeced you.

And the premises began to empty. They were thinning out

down on the floor and from the gallery one pair after another was going down the stairs.

The air was heavy with smoke, and the smell of beer lay thick and heavy over the tables with their deserted glasses.

There was no one up in the gallery but an elderly lady bobbing about and nodding seductively to Bai.

They had already turned the gas half down and Bai still sat there with his head in both his hands staring at the deserted, filthy main hall.

He swore roundly and rose.

The elderly lady was dodging around at the gate.

"Still here?" she said.

"Not bloody likely."

Bai vented all his fury in the push he gave the elderly lady.

"What on earth," the lady whined. "Is that the way to treat a lady, a woman who owns her own home?"

Kiær was in bed:

"Well," he said, "Did you have fun?"

Bai took his boots off.

"They didn't come," he said in a low voice.

"Rotten lot," said Kiær.

Bai undressed without speaking.

He lay there for a time with the light on. Then he put it out.

"Are you upset, old man?" said Kiær.

"Not really."

"Oh. Well, good night."

"But I'm getting old," said Bai. "Aye," he said again, slowly, "that's what it is."

Kiær turned over in bed, "Rubbish," he said. "But you go about it like a bull at a barn door, old man. You need to be in training, to be cock of the midden, and you need to take things slowly. Then you'll be all right. And able to enjoy yourself."

Kiær fell silent. It was not long before he was snoring. But Bai could not sleep. It was though he had the smell of beer in his nostrils for half the night, and he lay there tossing and turning.

The following morning, as he was packing his bags, Katinka's photograph fell out from between two handkerchiefs.

It was Mrs Abel who had packed it for him.

She had looked tenderly at it and packed it in tissue paper.

"That dear girl," she had said.

Louise, the last one, had been irritated: "Good heavens, why don't you give him a music box as well? So that he can play those 'dear melodies' of hers?"

Louise, the only one left at home, had a bad habit of snarling at her mother if she disapproved of something.

The widow had packed the portrait between the two handkerchiefs.

"He must have that bit of home with him."

Bai picked the portrait up from the floor and sat looking at it with eyes swimming with tears.

The Abels were at the station to meet Bai. The indoor rooms looked as though they had been spring-cleaned for Easter, with white curtains and a smell of cleaning in the air.

Bai sat on the sofa for his meal.

"It's nice to get back to your own home," he said. "At home in the nest."

He ate and drank as though he had not had a meal all the time he had been away.

Mrs Abel had tears in her eyes as she sat there looking fondly at "our homecomer".

He told them about his trip.

"The theatres," said the widow. "The season."

He had bought a gravestone. "Hell of a price."

"You don't have to think about that," said the widow, "the final act of love."

"Aye, that was what it was, as I said to Kiær, the final act of love," said Bai.

Louise never ran out of her small surprises. "You are not allowed to look," she said, holding her hand to his eyes while the widow took the lid off the latest dish of ragout.

"Yes, she has made such a lot of things," said the widow with a smile, "My elder daughter."

"We all like our home comforts," said Bai. He placed both his hands on the table and looked happy as he settled down for a quiet nap.

October arrived. There was quite a crowd on the platform waiting for the afternoon train. Little Jensen and all the Lindes and the family from the mill.

The widow was leaving to set up house for Ida, her younger daughter.

"Louise will be following on," she said as she threw her arms round her elder daughter's head. "She is happiest at home."

"She won't be coming until it's time for the wedding," she said.

The wedding was to be celebrated at the home of "my sister, the one who was married to a State Councillor".

"That is where they met," said the widow.

The train was announced. Bai came with a baggage claim slip and a ticket.

"He has been my providence," said the widow, nodding to him.

The train approached across the meadows.

"Give our love to Ida, then," said the old minister. "We will be thinking about her on the day."

"We know," said the widow. "We know where there are people who think kindly of us." She was moved and kissed the assembled company.

"Yes," she said, "this is a journey to say farewell."

The train was there. "Well, my dear Mrs Abel," said Bai. "It's time now."

"But what about my Louise?"

"We'll look after her." Bai had already pushed Mrs Abel into the carriage.

"Goodbye, Mrs Linde. Goodbye."

Louise jumped up on the running board and kissed her. "One last one," she said.

"Louise..." shouted the widow. The train had started to move.

Bai caught Louise, the only one the widow had left.

They waved their scarves and they waved their hands until the train was no longer in sight.

The Lindes walked along the road home with the family from the mill.

Louise wanted to have a look at something in the post bag and ran into the office in front of Bai. They laughed so loudly in there that it could be heard right out on the platform.

Little Miss Jensen had given up and was leaning against a post. The porter had moved the milk churns away from the platform and changed the points. And Miss Jensen stood there still, alone, leaning against her post.

The Lindes were at home.

The old minister was sitting with Agnes in the living room

while "Mother" saw to the tea.

It was growing dark. The old parson could hardly see Agnes as she sat at the piano.

"Sing a song for me," he said.

Agnes moved her hands a little, slowly up and down the keyboard. And then, quietly, in her dark contralto voice, she sang the song about Marianna:

> "Beneath the grassy grave is sleeping
> Our poor Marianna
> Come gather, girls, and join in weeping.
> Our poor Marianna."

Silence fell in the dark sitting room

The old minister folded his hands and dozed off.